For thirteen years now *Pe*
acknowledged to be the w
series. Originally publishe
the series has now appeare
the States.

CW01628411

Over five hundred *Perry R*
Continent and *Perry Rhodan* fan conventions are held annually. The first *Perry Rhodan* film, SOS From Outer Space has now been released in Europe.

The series has sold over *140 million* copies in Europe alone.

Also available in the *Perry Rhodan* series

ENTERPRISE STARDUST
THE RADIANT DOME
GALACTIC ALARM
INVASION FROM SPACE
THE VEGA SECTOR
THE SECRET OF THE TIME VAULT
THE FORTRESS OF THE SIX MOONS
THE GALACTIC RIDDLE

Kurt Mahr

Perry Rhodan 10

The Ghosts of Gol

Futura Publications Limited
An Orbit Book

An Orbit Book
First published in Great Britain in 1976
by Futura Publications Limited

Copyright © 1971 by Ace Books
An Ace Book by arrangement with Arthur Moewig Verlag

This series was created by Karl-Herbert Scheer and Walter Ernsting. This edition translated by Wendayne Ackerman and edited by Donald A. Wollheim.

This book is sold subject to the condition that it shall not, by way of trade or otherwise, be lent, re-sold, hired out or otherwise circulated without the publisher's prior consent in any form of binding or cover other than that in which it is published and without a similar condition including this condition being imposed on the subsequent purchaser.

ISBN: 0 8600 7869 8

Printed in Great Britain by
Richard Clay (The Chaucer Press), Ltd,
Bungay, Suffolk

Futura Publications Limited
Warner Road, London SE5

CONTENTS

1 Spooky Phenomena 7

2 Perils of Gol 24

3 Glowing – Beings? 43

4 The Valley of the Phantoms 60

5 Encounter with the Ghosts 75

6 A Message from the Unknown 89

7 Beyond the Galaxy 120

CHAPTER ONE

SPOOKY PHENOMENA

Rhodan's stern voice, resounding from the telecoms in all the corridors of the mighty spaceship, broke the quiet which had prevailed for several hours aboard the *Stardust II*.

'Commander to all Guppies! Prepare your ships for takeoff at nine-twenty ship time. I repeat ...'

The previous quiet had been deceptive. Beneath its surface, tension was growing, perhaps even fear, most certainly the disquieting realization of involvement with things beyond the comprehension of human brains. To the *Stardust's* crew of five hundred, never before had it been so apparent as in the past few days and hours to just what extraordinary degree the welfare of the entire ship depended on the capabilities of a single man.

A single man: Perry Rhodan.

Many of the men did not know the reasons for Rhodan's actions and the leader of the New Power did not deem it necessary to enlighten them. So rumours spread, at first ridiculed, then embellished with hair-raising details and finally accepted.

Rhodan's latest order meant new excitement for two hundred men of the crew. After the unnerving experience of hours of uncertain waiting, they preferred to plunge into the most dangerous adventure rather than remain inactive a moment longer.

Guppies were the eight auxiliary ships of the *Good Hope* class carried aboard the *Stardust II*. Nobody remembered who first called them such but 'Guppies' was now accepted as the common code name for the two hundred-foot-long ships.

The all clear reports for the Guppies had come. Perry Rhodan sat in the pilot seat in the Control Centre and listened to the telecom with an impassive face. He looked as if he were not interested in the chatter but after the eighth report he leaned over the mike and ordered:

'Proceed in accordance with the data of your automatic navigation control. Hold your ships in standby position in your respective target areas and scan the sector for structural changes. Keep your structure sensors manned at all times and report immediately any change in the space-time continuum. Start at prearranged time.'

With an abrupt move of his hand he switched off the telecom. He whirled around in his chair.

He was alone in the Command Centre with Reginald Bell, his companion ever since their first flight to Earth's moon and still his best friend on their way to the unknown.

Bell tried to smile but managed only a half-hearted grin. Cheerfulness seemed out of place these days.

'What do you anticipate?' asked Bell. 'Alien ships?'

Rhodan stared thoughtfully at him for a few seconds. Then he shook his head in vigorous negation and got up.

'No, no ships,' he answered.

Bell waited. He waited until he knew that Rhodan would give him no further explanation voluntarily.

'What in the devil else?' he asked gruffly. 'Am I supposed to guess or are you going to tell me?'

'I expect a structural disturbance,' Rhodan replied. 'How it will be brought about I don't know. The man we are chasing can change the space-time continuum at will.'

Bell laughed but he did not sound very cheerful.

'That *man*,' he mocked. 'I'd really like to see him. He probably has an energy spiral instead of a head and two machines where I have my arms.'

'We'll get to see him,' Rhodan said quietly. 'Then we'll find out whether he has a spiral or not.'

'Do you really believe that? I mean ...'

'Yes, I do,' interrupted Rhodan. 'I'm not fool enough to risk a deadly adventure against my better judgment.'

Bell mumbled something Rhodan did not understand. Then he asked:

'And our Guppies are supposed to determine in which region of space the disturbance will take place, right?'

'Exactly!'

Bell was silent for a while, then he made another effort.

'Listen, Chief, you've brought a metal cartridge from the past. What a fantastic feat – ten thousand years from the past! You've opened it and tried to decipher the text it contained. You're convinced that you've read it correctly, right? And this is what it said:

' "He who wishes to find the way can still turn back. But if he decides to go on, may it be known to him that he will receive no more help whatsoever. Soon a quake will shake space ..." and so on.

'So you drop out of sight for a few days and almost burn up the big positronic computer. Finally, you bring forth the great idea that you must send out all auxiliary ships to scour space for structural disturbances.

'If one takes into consideration that we cannot be at all sure that the translating machine is equipped to handle such complicated messages properly, don't you think that we've started something we cannot finish?'

Rhodan listened thoughtfully. Bell had become serious and Rhodan knew that he expected a serious answer.

'No, Bell,' Rhodan said quietly, emphasizing his words. 'I'm convinced that we can accomplish it.'

Bell's face changed from one second to the next. His mouth became firm and he cocked his head with its bristles of red hair.

'Well, come on, then, and tell it to the others too!' he growled.

'Which others?'

'Who on board this ship would dare oppose your commands – except the two Arkonides?'

For Captain Chaney the flight presented conflicting emotions. He commanded Guppy Number Five. He had taken off at nine-twenty ship time from *Stardust II* together with the seven other Guppies. He had set his automatic pilot on the course predetermined by Rhodan's calculations and had proceeded according to his instructions to a position which was no more than a distance of one astronomical unit from the orbit of the fifteenth Vega planet.

He stopped at this point and began to wait, conforming to his orders. At first he had thought that something was going to happen in the next few hours; but hours passed and nothing happened except that the fifteenth planet of Vega, which had been thirty million miles distant at his arrival, moved away a few more miles.

Captain Chaney stretched out and tried to sleep without much success. Then he got up again and stared with smarting eyes at the monitor screens of the optical scanners and structure field sensors.

Captain Chaney had not often had the opportunity to fly such a ship as this. He knew the ship very thoroughly but his knowledge stemmed more from his intensive hypo-training than from flying practice.

Chaney had piloted a few cruising flights in the Terrestrial solar system and this experience in itself had considerably affected his outlook. Only eighteen months before that event he had believed – while flying his supersonic jet plane as a first lieutenant – that it would be decades till man would reach Mars or Venus with his flaming rockets.

There were moments when he thought he was dreaming. At times he tried to convince himself that his experiences could not be real. Then an alarm signal would shrill or a range finder would begin to hum with blinking lamps— and he was back in reality again.

I am a dreamer, he thought, feeling tired.

'Orientation Section to Commander!' a harsh voice bellowed. 'Unidentified object on zero-one-eight degrees horizontal – two-six-six vertical.'

Chaney perked up. He moved the lines on the scale below the centre screen to 18 °H and 266 °V. The screen flickered and came to rest again. A glistening point showed up in its centre. It was changing its luminosity at regular intervals.

'What is that?' Chaney asked gruffly.

'Can't make it out, sir.'

'Velocity?'

'Fourteen miles per second, sir. Coming in our direction.'

'Minimum distance?'

'Eighteen miles, sir, in about forty minutes.'

Chaney waited. Eighteen miles was a small distance out in space. One should be able to recognize at eighteen miles what kind of an object with variable light intensity was drifting in space.

Forty minutes was a long time. Chaney kept looking till his eyeballs hurt but his observation screen was not sharp enough to make out the outline of the object.

Then the range finder reported again.

'False alarm, sir. It's the wreckage of a ship from the time of the Topide invasion; a Ferronian ship, sir.'

Chaney felt cheated.

'Okay,' he said with a tired voice.

Then he got up.

'Lieutenant Forge, take over my place. I'll go and catch some sleep. I guess it'll be a while till we get to see something real interesting.'

Rhodan established quiet with an imperious gesture of his hand.

'Let's start from the beginning,' he said bitterly, dividing his anger in equal measure between Khrest and Thora. 'You came to this sector of the galaxy on a search expedition in a cruiser which probably was the last one you had been able to launch on Arkon. You were hoping to find the mysterious world where the secret of perpetual cell reproduction had been discovered.

'Your expedition failed at first but now after some detours – which probably caused no more delay than if you had managed by yourselves – we are once more approaching our goal together.'

'In the vault underneath the Red Palace in Thorta we found some clues. We've made many great efforts to follow them up and we've found new clues. We're getting closer to our goal step by step and now you suddenly want to abandon everything! Why?'

The last word sounded like the crack of a whip. Bell, who was sitting nearby, winced. He could not remember ever having seen Rhodan so irate as during these past minutes.

Khrest did not reply. He held his long, narrow head lowered and stared at the floor. Thora had moved forward to the edge of her chair and looked at Rhodan. Hostility glared in her red eyes.

'I'll tell you why,' Rhodan continued, much calmer after a while, 'You are afraid!'

Khrest's white-haired head shot up.

'And if it were so?' he asked quietly. 'Do you think it's cowardly to be afraid in a situation like this?'

'Yes,' responded Rhodan, 'and you know why: because you've believed that the secret of eternal life can be cheaply obtained in the galaxy. You've been told that some unknown race has solved the puzzle and will be happy to let you in on the secret.

'But now it turns out that it just isn't so. The people who know the secret of cell preservation also know how to guard it. Whoever desires to learn it has to tangle with them according to their rules of the game.

'Since you have, after ten thousand years, a habit of

believing that everything has to fall into your lap, you now prefer to quit the game. One of these days, when we have more time, I'm going to tell you the fable of the Fox and the Sour Grapes.

'All I can tell you at the moment is that you're free to decide whether you want to await the outcome of our action in safety outside, or if you want to come along with us.'

Thora jumped up. Bell was holding his breath. He knew how Thora was given to acting on impulse and it looked for a moment as if she were ready to strangle Rhodan. She took a couple of steps towards Rhodan, then stopped and let her shoulders drop.

'Barbarian!'

Rhodan blunted the force of her fury by beginning to laugh.

'If it is barbarian to recognize necessities and civilized to be a coward, I would rather remain a barbarian.'

Khrest got up too.

'Will you give us a few hours to think about it?' he asked earnestly. 'The matter is important enough to be given serious consideration. I'm going to analyse your arguments carefully, Rhodan.'

'You'll have a few hours, providing our auxiliary ships don't report back earlier,' replied Rhodan.

Khrest nodded. Then he left the room, walking slowly. Thora hesitated.

'Have you already finished your deliberations?' Rhodan asked, taunting her.

She turned away and ran out. The automatic sliding door rolled with a hissing sound into its latches behind her.

Captain Chaney was awakened by a noise such as he had never heard before. After some effort and with the aid of two pills he had finally managed to fall asleep but he had no idea at the moment how long he had been in bed.

He got up and put his aching, ringing head under the water faucet in his cabin. As the water was rushing over his ears he heard the telecom start to blare:

'Attention, everybody, attention! This is your commander speaking. Alert ship for highest state of alarm! Stand by!'

Chaney snorted, wiped his face and stormed out of the cabin.

In the Command Centre Lieutenant Forge was still standing with the mike before his mouth.

'What's the matter?' shouted Chaney. 'Why didn't anyone wake me up?'

Forge showed the strict training he had enjoyed. He finished his message, put back the mike and stood at attention.

'Considerable structure changes in immediate vicinity. It's my opinion that a whole fleet of alien ships has appeared by hyper-transition.'

'Have you located them?'

'No, sir, not yet.'

Chaney remembered that a strange noise had aroused him from his sleep. Now it was no longer heard.

'What kind of a racket was that earlier?' he wanted to know.

Forge shrugged his shoulders and looked puzzled.

'I don't know, sir. Evidently the hull of the ship has been vibrating.'

'The ship vibrating!' shouted Chaney. 'Didn't you set up the protective screen?'

'I did, sir!'

'Then why, for heaven's sake . . .?'

He was almost thrown off his feet. The Command Centre began to sway violently and the material of which the walls were built squeaked in the joints. A spark flashed on the switch console of the copilot, followed by a black, malodorous cloud of smoke. The noise of the explosion could not be heard because the hull of the ship had begun to drone again.

Chaney recognized the sound as the same which had awakened him.

With shaky legs he walked over to his seat and called the Orientation Section.

'What's going on?' he yelled.

'Severe structure disturbances very close by, sir,' rasped the voice from the receiver.

'Find out where these disturbances have occurred and report the accurate distance of the location.'

The spooky phenomenon disappeared as quickly as it had come. The ship was settling down again. The droning stopped and Chaney was now able to walk straight on his legs. He went over to the seat of the copilot and examined the switch console. The explosion had shattered one of the measuring instruments into thousands of pieces and left nothing but a hole as big as a fist in the plastic surface.

'What kind of an instrument was that?' asked Chaney and pointed to the hole.

Forge came over.

'The dial of the small structure sensor, sir.'

Chaney suppressed a feeling of panic welling up in him. What sort of gravitational shocks could cause a structure sensor to burn out?

He turned away and ordered the radio technician to be ready with his hyper-communication set for a talk to Ferrol.

Before he could speak, however, he received another report from the range finder.

'The direction is zero-zero-eight degrees horizontal and one-eight-nine degrees vertical. Distance four-point-three astronomical units.'

'Can you make out anything in that area?'

'Yes, sir. The fourteenth planet of Vega.'

Chaney suddenly got the impression that his hyper-call had become very urgent. He barked at the radio officer to hurry up.

'We would like to talk to you,' said Khrest hesitantly, remaining in the hatch to keep it from immediately closing up again.

Rhodan nodded.

'Come on in!'

His anger had blown over long ago. He was feeling sorry for Khrest and all people like him. Thousands of years of comfort had made the race of the Arkonides forget how to jump over one's own shadow. To undertake any matter the result of which was not perfectly assured right from the start, appeared just as foolish to them as to shoot a full dose of neutron beams through one's head to see if one could survive it.

Thora entered the Command Centre behind Khrest.

Rhodan was sitting at a test stand and staring at a

metal cartridge which he had retrieved from the past during one of his previous actions. So far there was no hint that the capsule held anything other than the contents removed earlier, although Rhodan had no doubt that it did. It would have meant the end of the long tortuous road to eternal life if the great unknown person would furnish no more clues.

Rhodan swivelled around in his chair and looked attentively at the two Arkonides. Khrest was standing there, still undecided.

'Please sit down!' Rhodan smiled with amusement. 'This is your ship just as much as mine. Make yourself at home!'

Khrest sat. He seemed to have to force himself to speak as it took quite a while till he lifted his head and began.

'We've thought this matter over,' he started to say.

He got no further. At this moment many astonishing things began to happen almost simultaneously, which rendered totally insignificant what Khrest had decided about the situation.

The circular room reverberated with a sonorous droning which deafened the ears. Rhodan received such a strong jolt in his back that he swerved up from his chair.

He whirled around, his weapon half drawn but his moving body froze suddenly.

The metal cartridge on the test stand had begun to glow. It radiated a blue-white light, evidently without any attendant emission of heat since the surface of the table suffered no damage.

He noticed with amazement that the cartridge obviously radiated away its own matter. It became smaller and smaller as he watched and the light went out at the same time as the last bit of metal disappeared.

Rhodan let his hand drop and tried to peer through the wildly pulsating images which his overly agitated retina conjured up.

'Bell!'

'Yes, Chicf?'

'Call Tanaka. Tell him to come here at once!'

Bell reacted quickly and efficiently. He gave no sign whatsoever that the radiating cartridge had made any impression on him.

Bell was talking into the telecom mike when the high-pitched buzzing of the hycom set attracted Rhodan's attention. He leaped to the switchboard with two big jumps and adjusted the reception.

'Commander Rhodan speaking. Go ahead!'

'Guppy Number Five to Commander; Captain Chaney speaking. Strong structural changes in area of fourteenth planet, sir, coming in intervals. They are of such magnitude that I have trouble keeping the ship upright.'

'Any other observations?'

'No, sir. We've been unable to ascertain the cause of these disturbances.'

'All right. Thank you for your report. I'm signing off.'

He whirled around again.

'Where is Tanaka?'

'He's coming.'

Rhodan glanced at Khrest and Thora, who were frightened stiff in their seats. Khrest was still staring with wide open, unbelieving eyes at the test stand where the metal capsule had radiated away its substance in a blue-white light, and Thora remained motionless, covering her face with both hands.

The hatch rolled open and Tanaka Seiko entered the room. He was one of Rhodan's most capable mutants. Radioactivity had affected unused parts of his brain in such a manner that he could receive electromagnetic waves and understand their meaning if they were modulated as, for instance, radio waves.

During the last few days it had become apparent that Tanaka's sensitive brain did not only respond to electromagnetic influences but also reacted to others of a higher order.

Tanaka was stumbling as he came in. It seemed to take all his strength not to fall down. His face was so pale that it made the red scar on his cheek stand out. 'Did you understand it, Tanaka?' asked Rhodan sternly.

The Japanese nodded. Rhodan pointed to a chair.

'Sit down and tell us about it!'

'Somebody said, "You shall come now,"' Tanaka stammered. 'Then there was some talk about a warning. Yes, I understood. It said. "Remember the warning! Continue your search where the disturbance occurs."'

He paused and took a deep breath to overcome his exhaustion. Then he went on.

'Then it said: "Do not come without the higher knowledge! Nobody will help you, only the mountain will pulsate for you."'

Rhodan nodded and routinely rewound the tape on which he had recorded Tanaka's interpretation. He listened for a second time to what the Japanese had said and got up.

'"You shall come now,"' he murmured. 'But "Remember the warning. Continue your search where the disturbance occurs. Do not come without the higher knowledge. Nobody will help you, only the mountain will pulsate for you." '

It was a psychic message which was embedded in the metal cartridge, retrieved from the past by Rhodan and emitted at the exact moment the great unknown being had chosen.

I have to be careful not to lose my sanity, Rhodan reflected bitterly.

He could hear Tanaka panting beside him. The sound took his mind off his own thoughts. He looked at Bell, who was still waiting at the telecom. Bell reached hesitantly for the mike.

Rhodan nodded and took the mike over.

'Commander Rhodan speaking. Attention, everybody! Ship will take off in thirty minutes. All battle stations and range finders to be manned five minutes before start. All section chiefs to report when ready for action.

'Major Deringhouse and Major Nyssen, have both your space-fighter squadrons ready for launching at the airlocks.

'State of alarm number one as of now!'

The thirty minutes seemed to fly by. Khrest made a few attempts to speak but Rhodan averted him and asked for patience. Rhodan himself determined the course. The computer contained the orbit and velocity data of all planets of the Vega system in its memory bank. Rhodan elicited the information and received, in symbols of Arkonide mathematics, an equation for the course which was prepared for feeding into the automatic pilot.

Rhodan set the automatic pilot for ready start and took the all clear calls coming in one after another from all sections of the mighty ship.

Major Deringhouse was the last to come through with his report. He rattled it off and then inquired in a more personal tone, 'May I ask what's up?'

'Fourteen!' answered Rhodan curtly. 'We want to take a look at it.'

'Fourteen!' snapped Deringhouse. 'That monster?'

Rhodan nodded. 'That monster.'

Minutes later, the *Stardust II* lifted off. The huge spherical body with a diameter of twenty-five hundred feet threw a black shadow across the terrain, causing an unscheduled solar eclipse for a small area of Ferrol's surface.

This spectacle did not last very long. Roaring and trailing a glowing plume of ionized matter, the ship escaped into space. It was almost incredible for an observer contemplating the sight to see how quickly the tremendous ball shrank to a black point and vanished completely in one breath of air.

In the Command Centre of the ship Rhodan checked the light controls of the automatic pilot. They were blinking in the prescribed sequence and the right colours.

The course was steady. No transition had been planned. The flight would take one hundred and ten minutes.

Rhodan remembered that Khrest wanted to say something. He looked questioningly at the old Arkonide.

'Didn't you have a . . .?'

Khrest laughingly interrupted him. It was the first time in weeks that he really laughed.

'Oh yes, Perry, I had a request. I meant to tell you that we've thought the matter over and want to accompany you in any case.'

Rhodan looked startled.

'Right. Earlier, you hadn't made up your mind, I remember now.'

Thora got up. Her face twitched in a mixture of anger and gaiety.

'I'd just like to know what would have become of us if we *had* decided differently?' she asked bitingly.

'What luck that you didn't!' replied Rhodan with a smile.

CHAPTER TWO

PERILS OF GOL

The fourteenth Planet of Vega was an ammonia-methane giant of the Jupiter type. It was in this vicinity that Rhodan in the *Good Hope* had rescued Chaktor from the drifting wreckage of the Ferronian defence fleet which had been destroyed by the invading Topides.

This gigantic planet had three times the diameter of Jupiter, a staggering 260,000 miles, and, in contrast to Jupiter, an enormous density. According to the information given by Ferronian astronomy the gravitation on the surface amounted to more than nine hundred G's, which meant that a man there would have to carry more than nine hundred times his weight.

Rhodan, however, believed that this figure was too high and had it checked as the *Stardust II* approached the planet. Nine hundred G's would mean that single actions of the eight auxiliary ships, or even space-fighters, would be impossible above the methane-ammonia world. The auxiliary ships had the capacity of neutralizing five hundred G's. If the gravitation exceeded that they had to utilize the help of their drive engines, which in turn reduced their mobility.

The planet was a monster in every respect. Long distance measurements determined that the height of the atmosphere was amost twelve thousand miles above the core itself, which could be either solid or liquid. The pressure on the surface, therefore, far exceeded anything human high pressure technology had invented or produced.

As *Stardust II* approached the planet within one astronomical unit, Rhodan received the result of the gravitation measurements. The gravitational force prevailing on the surface was nine hundred and sixteen G's, nine hundred and sixteen times as much as the weight on Earth.

Thereupon Rhodan ordered his Guppies, the eight auxiliary ships, to return to Ferrol and to wait there for further developments. Then he called his senior officers and the two Arkonides for a briefing.

Anyone who believed that Rhodan would permit a discussion was disappointed. Rhodan stood in front of his officers and announced his decisions.

'The venture is very dangerous,' he said with a harsh voice. 'Let's not have any illusions about that. We're running the risk of losing our ship.

'On the other hand we must keep in mind what has so far been done in this undertaking. We're dealing with somebody who will entrust his secret only to those he considers worthy to receive it.

'The probability that a serious mishap will occur is, in my opinion, very slight. One doesn't test the courage of a candidate with the intention of destroying him.

'But we must take every precaution. The unknown informed us that we must rely on our own strength. I have no doubt that our strength will prove superior to anything at all we might encounter on this planet.'

He paused and waited for objections. There were none.

'Certain technical details will have to be considered,' he continued. 'We need vehicles in which we can operate adequately on the surface. These vehicles have to sustain a pressure of fifty thousand atmospheres and must be neutralized against the gravitation of nine hundred and sixteen G's. Keep in mind that the safety of the personnel depends on the care with which these precautionary measures are taken.

'We have a few hours to prepare for these requirements. Then we'll be beyond the point of no return. Thank you!'

Everybody was dismissed with the exception of Khrest and Thora. Bell, whose post was in the Command Centre, also remainded.

'Do you know what you are doing?' asked Khrest.

'He never thinks before he acts,' Thora broke in. 'He simply does it and most of the time he's lucky.'

'I've considered everything,' Rhodan answered Khrest. 'I'm risking the ship to search for the secret of eternal life. Don't you agree that it's worth more than this ship?'

'True enough,' admitted Khrest. 'But what good will the secret do us if we get stuck on this monster?'

'Stuck? One of our auxiliary ships can rescue us, if . . .'

'Rescue us? Against a gravitation of nine hundred and sixteen G's?'

'Well, it'll be a difficult manoeuvre. But those ships can be steered remotely from a far distance so that not even one of the robots has to be exposed to this gravitation. We, however . . .'

'We, however,' criticized Thora, 'have five or six safe vehicles at best for three hundred men. There'll be room for twenty or thirty more in each vehicle. What about the others?'

'The others won't have to worry any more about being picked up. Isn't that what you wanted to hear?' answered Rhodan dryly.

Thora made no further reply. Rhodan continued to exasperate her.

'Besides, you assured me only an hour ago that you wanted to share in this expedition. Does this mean that you've changed your mind again in the meantime?'

'No, you stubborn mule!' snarled Thora angrily and marched out.

'We ought to call it Gol,' said Bell pensively.

'What?'

'That,' responded Bell, pointing his open hand towards the visiscreen across which storms in the uppermost layers of the atmosphere were raging. 'Isn't Gol an abominable ogre in some old legend?'

'Could be,' answered Rhodan, lost in thought.

Stardust II hovered eleven thousand miles above the actual surface of the planet according to the micro-wave probe. The ship approached on the day-side of the planet and the temperature in the immediate neighbourhood of the *Stardust* rose to 120 °F under the influence of the direct radiation from the blue-white giant star Vega.

The rotation period of the planet was calculated to be close to fourteen hours. This meant that the fast rotating surface created uninterrupted storms in the border strata next to it – storms under a pressure of more than forty thousand atmospheres!

Rhodan tried to imagine the sort of being who would select such a world to stage his trial. It was beyond his comprehension.

'Nine thousand miles,' a steady voice reported on the telecom.

Following the custom on Earth, on board the *Stardust* and all other ships, distances were stated in miles and feet unless they were on the order of interstellar dimensions.

Still nine thousand above the surface.

'Wind velocity thirteen hundred feet per second,' another voice announced.

Bell started to laugh. But he did not sound very cheerful.

'Wind velocities greater than the speed of sound,' he mumbled. 'What is that going to do to us?'

Rhodan answered seriously:

'The velocity of sound depends on the substance and the density through which it travels. Here we have a mixture of ammonia and methane and the density far exceeds the atmosphere on Earth. Therefore, the speed of sound is much greater than in air under normal pressure.'

Bell started to reply but the warning buzz of an instrument interrupted him.

The red warning light of the structure sensor glared like the eye of a witch. Rhodan studied the confusing pattern of impulses on the oscillograph screen of the sensor.

Normally, the oscillograph reacted to a structure change in space with a green point of light formed on the screen. The location of the point on the grid of the co-ordinates indicated where in space the change occurred.

However, the picture Rhodan saw at present was a wobbly, chaotic pattern originating at a central point and spreading over the whole screen. Rhodan was unable to make any sense out of the pattern.

He knew that the structure sensor recorded its images on a tape to preserve them. For that reason he took time to observe the peculiar play of lines until it suddenly disappeared again.

The attached chronometer registered that the sensor had been activated for sixteen seconds.

Rhodan had a short talk with Tanaka Seiko over the telecom but Tanaka had not noticed anything. If these playful structure changes in space had any significance at all it was hidden in gravitational shocks to which Tanaka was not sensitive.

The game had become a shade more difficult.

'Seven thousand,' said the navigator.

Rhodan removed the tape produced by the structure sensor and projected it. He magnified the picture ten times and studied it once more without arriving at any conclusions.

However, he determined the co-ordinates of the point of origin and changed the course in that direction. In this manner they crossed the night and day border line and now moved through the swirling, stormy darkness.

The temperature outside the ship's hull had sunk to 200° absolute or – 260 °F.

'Six thousand miles!'

At the same moment the structure sensor reacted once

again. It did so in the same manner as the first time: it drew green lines in a senseless pattern all over the screen, toying for sixteen seconds with Rhodan's reasoning theories and then fading away.

Only one thing was different: the central point of the line pattern was at the point of origin of the co-ordinates themselves. The *Stardust* was located exactly vertically above the emitter and there could be no doubt that the source was situated on the surface of the giant planet.

Rhodan compared the two visitapes with each other. There was no time to evaluate the comparison but one thing that seemed to be certain was that the two patterns did not to differ except for the location of the central point.

This indicated that the space structure change which was taking place below the *Stardust* was intentional and not an accidental, statistical occurrence. This was also suggested by the duration of the disturbance which lasted sixteen seconds in both cases.

The navigator called.

'Below us is an obscure area, sir. Appears to be a mountain. Differences in height up to sixty thousand feet. The terrain is most unsuitable for a landing.'

'Can you make out a more favourable place?'

'Yes, sir. About one hundred and twenty miles from here is a mirror-like surface, if I can trust my instruments.'

'Correct our course. But deviate as little as possible from our present direction.'

The navigator determined the co-ordinates of the new landing area and transmitted the programme data for the course correction to the automatic pilot. The reception of this information was signalled in the Command Centre and Rhodan, who was flying the *Stardust* only semi-automatically because of the difficult landing procedure, set the new course.

At the altitude of six hundred miles it became necessary to increase the power of the generators for the protective screen to the highest level. The storm which whipped the mass of ammonia and methane with unbelievable velocity began to interfere with the ship's course. The huge sphere of the *Stardust* was pushed about and only the highest energy level of the protective screen was sufficient to prevent the storm from unbalancing the ship.

A strange phenomenon was now observed on the visiscreen. Methane, one of the two main ingredients of the planet's atmosphere, becomes easily ionized. The ionized molecules of the gas bombarded the protective screen and enveloped the *Stardust* in a glowing halo which trailed behind in immense spirals.

It was impossible to determine the nature of the atmosphere. The enormous pressure caused the ammonia and methane molecules to form a dense mixture which normally would result in a liquid. But by definition the liquid state requires a surface formed by the fluid itself. The atmosphere lacked such a surface and Rhodan had to conclude that they had found a region here of super-high pressures and low temperatures still unknown to Terrestrial thermodynamics due to the absence of opportunities for such experiments on Earth.

In the meantime the structure sensor had responded three more times. The observation screen showed the same pattern, the reception period again lasted sixteen seconds and by now Rhodan had ascertained that the intervals between the transmissions were always the same.

Transmissions!

Somebody was present in the neighbourhood of the mountain peak of which, so the navigator claimed, was twelve miles above the normal level and was sending the same space-warping effects which occurred at the transition of a spaceship. They were unwanted side effects which could not be controlled by mankind.

We have to find a different name for these other beings, Rhodan thought; after all, one could not call all those who were intelligent, mankind.

The transmissions were sent by somebody who was also able to modulate their effects as was shown by the pattern on the oscillograph screen. Rhodan began to understand why Khrest and Thora wanted to abandon their original plan. Some power was at work here which was far superior to the Arkonides.

'Altitude three hundred and sixty miles!'

'Outside temperature eighty-five degrees absolute.'

'The day has begun, sir, at least according to our calculations. Can you recognize anything?'

Rhodan chided, 'Do you expect radiant sunshine at the bottom of an ammonia ocean twelve miles deep?'

More reports came in. They were rife with the anxiety which was gripping the men. There was hardly anyone who was immune to the influence which this utterly strange world exerted. It did not help matters that most of the crew had no direct view at the outside. The navigators and the men at the battle stations relied on the range finder screens, which depicted solid objects as monochromatic points, lines or planes. Nobody knew what it really looked like outside.

Rhodan could have consoled them. On the screens of the visual monitoring system there was merely a black-grey spread without contours or details.

Bell stared at the automatic calendar.

Terrestrial time prevailed on board the *Stardust*. Rhodan had made this decision not only out of sentimentality but because any time was as useful and practical as another on the far-flung flights of the *Stardust*.

'December seventh, eighteen-twenty hours,' said Bell. If the slight melancholy in his voice could not be detected it was only because of the more preponderant anxiety. 'At this time I am ...'

'Two hundred and forty miles!'

'... and at this time I am ...'

'Wind velocity twenty-one hundred feet per second, sir. Remaining constant for last ten minutes.'

'... at this time ...'

'Navigator to Commander. The surface below us does not appear as smooth as before. I don't see any explanation for it.'

'Can you describe the change?'

'Yes, sir. It looks as if a meadow has suddenly turned into a sea.'

'That's it. At the surface of the planet, the temperature is near the melting point of methane. A slight rise in temperature is sufficient to turn the frozen methane into a liquid. Make a depth probe of the density. I want to find out how deep the methane has melted.'

'Yes, sir.'

And barely a minute later:

'I found solid ground thirty feet below the undulating surface.'

'All right. No change of course!'

Bell sighed sadly and gave up his attempt to tell what he would have done on Earth at this time. He turned his attention to his instruments.

The control light of the protective screen began to flicker. Bell responded before Rhodan noticed it.

'Copilot to Protective Screen Generator. What's the matter with the screens? Why don't you shift to full power?'

'The generators are running under full power, sir,' replied the engineer resentfully.

'Stabilize the ship! The screen is out of control.'

Rhodan reacted in his own way. He reduced the thrust of the engines and lowered the ship at an accelerated pace. If anything happened to the protective screen, he preferred to be on solid ground.

Solid ground!

'Attention! Ship is touching down!'

Rhodan stood with concentrated attention before the huge pilot switch panel. The automatic steering had taken over the task of probing the bottom and switching off the engines, or rather adjusting them to minimum output, as soon as adequate contact had been made.

The methane was liquid up to a depth of thirty feet and beneath it was a treacherous strata. At sixty feet the landing pads of the hydraulic legs found enough support so that the generators were turned down by the automatic control.

The humming which had pervaded every last corner

of the *Stardust*, and to which everybody's ears had become readily accustomed, died down to almost nothing so that all became aware of the quiet.

Rhodan set a limit switch to govern the generators in order to prevent the gravity value from sinking below nine hundred and sixteen G's. The gravity neutralizers together with the engines kept the *Stardust* in a weightless state even after the landing. The support legs had found solid ground but they did not depend on it. Rhodan was sure that the ship could take off anytime he desired.

He posted three guards at every generator and explained to them with great emphasis that the safety of the ship and its crew depended upon the engines being ready to start at any moment.

The incident which had occurred at two hundred and forty miles altitude had made him very apprehensive. A few seconds after Bell's talk to the protective screen engineer the screen had become stable again. But the phenomenon remained inexplicable. There was no apparent reason why the intensity had fluctuated for half a minute.

The engineer assured him that the adjustment had remained untouched. The protective screen generators were controlled from a central switch panel which had been under the watchful eyes of the engineer at all times.

They could find no explanation for the incident.

'It looks as if somebody on the outside has tapped our screens,' speculated Bell.

The idea was absurd. But the incident was of such a nature as to cause all sorts of absurd thoughts.

'I would like to ask you to examine the record of the structure sensors,' said Rhodan gravely. 'It looks as if some kind of a message might be hidden in these structure changes. Tanaka Seiko was unable to detect anything. That leaves only the structure sensor to be studied.'

Khrest nodded thoughtfully.

'Do you have any clues?' he asked.

Rhodan shook his head. Only later did it occur to him that this was the first time Khrest had asked his advice on a technical matter.

'No, not the slightest. Unless you want to call what we so far know about the mentality of the stranger a hint.'

'Well, that doesn't give me much to go by.'

Khrest stared dejectedly at the narrow plastic picture strips which were lying on the table in front of him.

'And what do you intend to do?' he finally asked.

'The technicians have built an exploration vehicle with remote control. I'll have it tested outside. If it performs according to expectations, I'll drive it myself and look around.'

'Out there?' Khrest pointed his thumb over his shoulder.

Khrest shook his head.

'Sometimes it makes me shudder when I sense your ambition. Don't you have any fear?'

'Plenty,' assured Rhodan with a grin.

'Everything is satisfactory, sir. The car was outside for three hours and was driven around about thirty miles. The screen generators are functioning faultlessly as well as the remote steering. If you pass out somewhere we can always bring you back home.'

'Thank you,' said Rhodan with an appreciative smile.

The 'car' was a monstrous vehicle. To begin with it had

been hopeless to build it like a glider to move above ground. The extreme gravity of Gol – Rhodan had accepted the name – forbade such experiments at the outset. Therefore, it moved on caterpillar tracks. The technicians had adapted the chassis of one of the robot work machines. Only thirty per cent of the vehicle's volume could be utilized. A small compartment held the engine and almost seventy per cent of the space was required for the protective screen generators which had to protect the vehicle from the incapacitating gravity.

For the sake of his own safety, Rhodan would have preferred to have the car tested more thoroughly. But he had no time to lose in this enterprise. The unknown individual had very definite ideas as to how much time it should take for a man to solve his mysteries to be considered worthy of him. So far no one knew what time he had allotted for the solution of the Gol enigma.

Bell had insisted that he accompany Rhodan on his first trip but Rhodan refused his request.

'You must never forget that you're the only man, except myself, who has acquired the entire knowledge of the Arkonides. Mankind cannot afford to lose both of us at the same time.'

Instead, he selected Major Deringhouse and the Japanese Tanaka Seiko as his companions.

The tractorlike vehicle was driven out through the lowest lock of the *Stardust*, which was at a normal landing level with the ground. Rhodan steered it himself. The observer screen which served to find him his bearing was coupled with an infra-red searchlight. Its invisible, highly concentrated beam penetrated the darkness on Gol's surface more than half a mile and thus provided sharp and clear pictures on the screen.

Major Deringhouse handled the regular microwave range finder whereas Tanaka Seiko served as radioman for the time being.

Rhodan watched on the all-round screen the closing of the huge doors of the ship locks behind the 'caterpillar'. Meanwhile liquid methane had flowed into the locks and evaporated in the warm surroundings. The dangerous gas was pumped out and rose in great bubbles through the sea of methane in which the vehicle was striving to gain solid ground.

Rhodan made a complete sweep with the searchlight and saw that the carrier was indeed floating like a submarine. The upper boundary of the ellipsoid-shaped antigrav-screen still had twenty-five feet of liquid methane above.

Rhodan tried to picture what would happen if the temperature suddenly dropped and the methane became solid.

However, the difficulty of steering diverted him from all these useless speculations. The viscosity of the ground was so sluggish that the caterpillar tracks were ineffective unless all available power was turned on. This way the vehicle made about twenty miles per hour.

Rhodan followed a direction which, according to magnetic measurements on board the *Stardust*, had been defined as south. There in the south was the mountain range in which the transmitter of the inexplicable pattern on the visiscreen of the structure sensor was situated.

After about fifteen minutes the ground began to rise.

The height of the liquid methane above the carrier decreased. Tanaka transmitted the first of his routine reports to the ship. It was perfectly received and confirmed.

A few minutes later the vehicle emerged from the sea of methane. The generators howled as they climbed up the steep shore.

Rhodan stopped and rotated the searchlight all around.

'Take a look at that!' he exclaimed.

He had stopped the searchlight and illuminated a lonely, needle-shaped rock which jutted high out of the terrain. It stood no more than six hundred feet away from the shore of the lake from which they had just now emerged. The diameter at the bottom measured about fifteen feet. The needle was tapered and formed a sharp point at a height of about three thousand feet.

'What is that?' wondered Deringhouse. 'It's moving, isn't it?'

Nobody answered.

Indeed, the needle moved. It seemed to contract. It became visibly smaller and the circumference was reduced at the same speed. Rhodan looked at his watch. After scarcely six minutes the needle vanished completely. Where there had been a fabulous rock formation a glistening plain stretched unbroken to the mountain chain twelve miles in the distance.

Rhodan started up again.

'What was that?' groaned Deringhouse.

Rhodan smiled at him.

'An icicle,' he said above the purring engines.

Deringhouse stared at him uncomprehendingly.

'Frozen methane,' explained Rhodan. 'It looks like a regular piece of rock. But when the temperature rises above the melting point of methane it disappears slowly. If you looked closely you could see rivulets of methane flowing in all directions.'

Half an hour later they had reached the foothills. In the meantime they had encountered a number of different rock formations which vanished before their eyes.

The scenery was in motion. In Rhodan's opinion there existed nothing except frozen methane or ammonia in the immediate surroundings. Therefore, everything was subject to the transforming effects of minor temperature changes.

Rhodan realized the difficulties of orientation created for those who travelled in such a world. The only safe way to proceed was to follow a set of co-ordinates. Rhodan told Tanaka to report to *Stardust II* accordingly.

The question remained: the mountain where the mysterious transmissions originated – of what did it consist? It was improbable that such tremendous formations were created spontaneously from masses of the frozen atmosphere. It had to be assumed that part of the true surface of Gol was protruding there and that it underwent far fewer translations.

'... only the mountain will pulsate for you ... !'

Rhodan remembered the last sentence of the strange message which Tanaka Seiko had translated.

One did not call something a mountain unless it really was a mountain.

With churning tracks the vehicle swung slowly around a foothill.

The slopes of the hills reflected the typical infrared glimmer which Rhodan had noticed everywhere – ice and snow.

Behind the hill there was another stretch of level terrain. But farther back a wall of rock rose up almost vertically. It did not look very inviting. There seemed to be neither a crack nor a gap. The wall was so solid that Rhodan began to search for ways of circumventing the obstacle.

As he was sweeping the beam of his searchlight he reduced the speed of his vehicle. The spot of light moved hundreds of yards over the wall and suddenly disappeared.

Rhodan was baffled and repeated the search again. Slowly the beam moved across the wall and disclosed the normal cracks, crevices and chinks in rocks.

Then, by advancing merely one more degree, the light became extinguished. There was no indication that it had reached the end of the wall and that the beam was shining the full length of its range into the grey night of Gol.

The wall was still there but the searchlight made no visible mark on it.

Rhodan had no time left to wonder. The little fusion-aggregate from which the searchlight drew its energy suddenly started to hum. Rhodan bent forward to see what had happened. From the connection of the aggregate to the searchlight switch on the control panel crackled a foot-long blue spark. The stench of burning insulation pervaded the interior of the carrier for a while until it was pumped out. The searchlight was completely extinguished and a red light on the switchboard lit up to signal that the searchlight was defective.

Rhodan recognized the danger of the situation. From now on he would be forced to proceed in darkness. The radar did not distinguish very clearly between the atmosphere and the obstacles of methane and ammonia ice which presented the greatest difficulties.

Rhodan turned the vehicle around.

Deringhouse and Seiko had watched the incident without reaction. Neither of them seemed to understand the dilemma they faced through the failure of the searchlight. Rhodan did nothing to enlighten them. They would discover it soon enough when the first icicle collapsed on the vehicle and bombarded it with chunks of congealed gas.

CHAPTER THREE

GLOWING – BEINGS?

'I don't have the faintest idea how to decipher this,' said Khrest disgustedly and switched off the projector.

'The unknown we are chasing must have a warped sense of humour.'

Bell shrugged his shoulders.

'What do you expect? He's guarding a very precious secret. If we want to obtain it we shouldn't let the eccentricity of its keeper deter us. Won't you try once more?'

Khrest sighed.

He started to return to his projector but after two steps he stumbled and had to throw himself across a chair to keep from falling to the ground.

Bell had lost his footing at the same moment. He threw up his arms and tried to balance himself before he crashed with his broad back against the switch panel of the radio officer.

Alarm sirens wailed through the quiet of the Command Centre.

Khrest got up and studied the floor of the Command Centre carefully. He looked around and found on one of the tables a small plastic cylinder, narrow and long like a pencil, which served as a test probe for tube lines. He put it on the floor and rotated it. Finally he let go.

The little cylinder started to move. Gaining speed, it

rolled across the smooth floor and came to rest at the wall.

'That's what I thought,' exclaimed Khrest. 'The ship is leaning over!'

Bell went into action. He quickly dialled and within seconds got the engineer in charge of the protective screen on the telecom.

'I'm about to regain control, sir,' the engineer reported hastily, shouting loud enough so that Bell could hear him in spite of the wailing sirens. 'As far as I can tell, two gravity generators were running idle momentarily. As a result the neutralization screen became weak or failed completely on one side. That's why we toppled over.'

'Were idle?' shouted Bell. 'Are you trying to tell me that they're operating normally again?'

'Yes, sir!'

Bell ended his call. At the same time the wailing of the sirens ceased. Bell went over to the pilot compartment and examined the reports. There could be no doubt that the ship was leaning. The support leg had sunk more than sixty feet into the ground and the inclination of the vessel floors measured in excess of one degree.

The correction of the situation was no problem for Bell. He could increase the power of the engines by the proper amount to raise the ship to its normal level and then revert to the previous output. He took the necessary steps and determined that everything was functioning as it was supposed to. The incident was a mysterious manifestation which was gone as quickly as it had come.

His inability, however, to find an explanation for the failure of the generators upset Bell very much. Even though he possessed the entire knowledge of the Arkonides he did not succeed in detecting the reason for the interruption of two faultlessly operating gravity generators which functioned perfectly again after a few seconds.

Khrest looked at him, downcast, and asked: 'You don't understand it either?'

Bell shook his head angrily.

'No,' he said, 'I don't have the foggiest idea.'

The telecom signal interrupted them.

'Observer to Commander! Please inspect screen C, sir. I believe you'll be interested in the sighting.'

Bell turned on the visiscreen with curiosity.

The screen lit up. Dark grey flickering spread all over it.

'I see . . .' began Bell.

'Nothing,' he wanted to say but at this moment he did see something. It was a dimly glowing, shapeless image which moved like a veil through the grey murkiness. It looked like a light trail of smoke or . . .

Bell knew no comparison for it. However, it was something else which impressed him most about the glowing form.

Out there where the light patch cavorted reigned wind velocities and pressures which were beyond human imagination. Smoke or nebulous formations – or whatever the thing out there resembled – would have been torn apart or blown away in seconds by the continuous storm.

The patch outside, however, was swaying, stretching out and contracting again. It did not seem to be affected at all by the raging atmosphere of Gol.

Bell stared at the patch until it disappeared.

'Thank you,' said Bell weakly to the observation

officer. 'Keep an eye on it.'

He avoided looking at Khrest and stared at the floor instead.

Khrest said after a while, 'I don't know if it's worth racking our brains about it. The aerodynamic conditions in this atmosphere are so strange that all sorts of symptoms can occur. They look very mysterious and defy explanation at first but could turn out to be quite simple.

'For instance, the phenomenon we've just observed could be an exotic form of an electric discharge similar to a thunderstorm.'

Bell nodded.

'Yes, of course,' he said absentmindedly. 'If you regard the glowing patch alone. But if you consider that a few moments ago two of our generators acted up in a puzzling manner, what conclusion would you draw then?'

Waving his hand, he continued: 'I know what you're going to say. It could be a coincidence, right?'

'You know what? We'll wait a little. If methodical forces are at work here we'll experience them again more frequently. So far they don't appear to have sufficient energy to constitute a danger.'

He looked at the clock.

'Another report from the vehicle is due,' he murmured.

It came a few moments later.

Tanaka Seiko reported that the infrared searchlight had conked out and that their vehicle was attempting to find its way home in blindness. Rhodan requested a radio beam signal to guide them back.

Bell gave the order for the radio beam signal. Then he

turned to Khrest.

'Thunderstorms all over the place,' he said, sneering a little. 'The searchlight has been struck by lightning, too.'

The observation screen was almost useless. None the less, Rhodan had not switched it off. While the vehicle steered carefully in the direction of the radio impulses coming from the *Stardust* he stared, lost in thought, at the shapeless grey world outside.

He knew that he could not recognize an ice needle even if he were close to it. Gol's atmosphere was so dense that it absorbed the brightest sunrays in a fraction of an inch.

'The guide signals are getting weaker, sir,' announced Deringhouse.

Rhodan recognized the effect. He stopped the vehicle and backtracked until Deringhouse reported that the signals were coming again with normal intensity. Then he turned right and drove forward once more. The vehicle moved at a snail's pace.

Deringhouse said reassuringly, 'We're all right. We can go on.'

It turned out that the guide signals reacted more sensitively to obstacles than Deringhouse's scanners which could barely distinguish between liquid, gaseous or solid methane. As soon as an obstacle arose between the *Stardust* and the vehicle the radio impulses became weaker. Deringhouse had not paid any attention the first time and Rhodan had run into a rock of methane ice, fortunately at slow speed. Since then Deringhouse watched the intensity of the signal carefully.

Tanaka Seiko was sitting at his telecom set. He received the guide signals clearly and was even able to differentiate changes of intensity, although not as accurately as Deringhouse's measuring instruments.

That was all Tanaka could hear. Except for the radio impulses there was only the usual static in the atmosphere.

There was nothing else. Really nothing?

Tanaka asked himself if the peculiar hum stemmed indeed from atmospheric disturbances. The intensity of such disturbances was normally fluctuating, sometimes stronger and sometimes weaker following the laws of statistics.

He observed such changes here too. But he noticed an additional strange humming of constant amplitude.

He was thinking about calling Rhodan's attention to it when the hum suddenly grew to a roar which caused his head to ache.

At the same moment Rhodan jumped up.

The grey observation screen showed a bright spot. Small and apparently spherical at first, it soon became bigger and spread in all directions.

Rhodan stopped the vehicle with a jerk.

'Sir!' moaned Tanaka.

'Yes?'

'I'm receiving something. Roaring, rather loud. It's busting my head!'

'Don't let it get you,' growled Rhodan. He continued staring at the spot.

He got an idea. He removed the infrared filter from the receiving tube and saw that the spot disappeared. Then he put the filter back in and the spot became visible once more.

'Infrared,' murmured Rhodan.

Deringhouse rotated his scanning antenna.

'I'm not getting any reflect,' he reported. 'But . . .'

A dim flickering spread over the observation screen. The light spot remained immobile. The new light came from a different source. It was the most intense in the upper half of the right edge of the screen.

It was the place where Deringhouse's antenna was located.

'Turn it off!' shouted Rhodan.

With a quick jab Deringhouse switched off the scanner. The glowing became weaker and soon disappeared altogether.

However, the spot had become bigger and brighter.

'Your antenna was glowing,' said Rhodan, without taking his eyes off the observation screen.

Deringhouse gave no answer. It was impossible for an antenna to glow. But then he himself had seen the effect on the screen.

'I'm going after it,' said Rhodan with a hoarse voice. 'Deringhouse, watch the guide signals!'

The motor began to whir and the vehicle started with a jolt. The mysterious light spot came closer and closer. At least that appeared to be the case at first. However, after a certain time, the spot did not change its size any more. It seemed to retreat at the same rate with which the carrier tried to approach it.

Rhodan drove a few hundred yards and stopped.

'It's useless,' he grumbled in disappointment. 'It's leading us around by the nose. Maybe it's purpose is to lead us astray. Deringhouse, what's our direction?'

'Zero-zero-eight degrees, sir.'

'Any trouble?'

'Not that I know of.'

'Distance?'

'One mile and a quarter to go, sir.'

It took almost half an hour to traverse this distance.

When he finally immersed the vehicle into the sea of methane, Rhodan felt as though he had reached a haven. He was diving in with his cumbersome vehicle in a flourish and drove it straight to the lock where Bell had set up a powerful searchlight.

After the gates of the lock had been closed behind the vehicle and the big pumps exchanged the dangerous methane for breathable air, they knew they had survived the perilous journey.

A little fatigued, they clambered out of the vehicle, entered the antigrav elevator to go up and gratefully stepped into the Command Centre within two minutes.

Rhodan stood with his back towards his listeners. They were Bell, Khrest, Thora and the two majors, Deringhouse and Nyssen.

'I think your electrical thunderstorm theory is excellent, Khrest,' said Rhodan. 'Although only'—here he turned around on his heel and faced the Arkonide—'for the purpose of reassuring the crew.

'Ourselves, we know that these things don't happen accidentally.'

'Is that so?' questioned Khrest. 'How do we know that?'

Rhodan explained obligingly. 'Tanaka tells us that the spot of light which we observed in the vehicle emitted hyper-radiation. Tanaka can differentiate between hyper-radiation and simple electromagnetic radiation by the manner in which these painful symptoms affect him. There is no such thing as an electromagnetic beam which emits hyper-radiation.'

He was pacing back and forth. His listeners followed him with attentive eyes.

'Another thing,' continued Rhodan. 'Something out there ruined our searchlight. I had the distinct impression that the energy was literally sucked out of the fusion-aggregate. The line was thereby overloaded and burned up.

'A few minutes later we encountered in the solitude of Gol a glowing being which emitted infrared rays exactly in the same region of the spectrum as our searchlight. Besides ...'

'Aren't you a little rash?' interrupted Thora. 'Glowing being! Do you mean to say that these things are life forms?'

'Wait a minute!' begged Rhodan. 'We have some more facts. Deringhouse attempted to get this thing into his range finder. It created no reflex on the observation screen but his antenna began to glow. I'm convinced that we'd have had the same result as with the searchlight if Deringhouse hadn't switched off the scanner in time.'

He stood before his listeners and looked at them one after the other, his hands clasped behind his back. When he started to talk again, he did so with a harsh and forceful voice.

'There's only one reasonable explanation for all these incidents we've experienced, from the fluctuation in our protective screen shortly before our landing to the glowing of Deringhouse's range finder antenna. Something or somebody on this planet has the capability of absorbing energy of any kind and is making exorbitant use of it.'

There was a long silence. Too long for Reginald Bell.

'Are we supposed to think,' he let loose, 'of this something or somebody as a living or perhaps intelligent being?'

Rhodan smiled.

'This is a problem with which we'll have to wrestle. The answer can't be stated in a few words and it won't make it easier to understand.

'Tanaka has ascertained that these beings emit hyper-radiation. However, nothing can emit hyper-radiation unless it belongs, at least partially, to a higher order of space.

'It would be violating the spirit of scientific clarity to *imagine* something about these forms. All we know is that they're here. We can study them when we have the opportunity and, if we're lucky, we'll eventually be in a position to describe their existence with symbols of Arkonide mathematics.

'That's all.

'Please go back to your stations. We'll have to examine this matter and make a few calculations. I'll notify you in case anything of importance happens.'

Nyssen and Deringhouse got up and left. Reginald Bell did not move. Khrest started to rise but sank back with a sigh against the bolster. Thora looked at Rhodan with big red eyes.

'You ought to be more careful,' she said pensively. 'You're talking to your men about beings living in a higher order of space. I'm not sure whether these people, although they're majors, are familiar enough with the concepts of hyper-geometry to know that there's no value judgment expressed by that.'

Rhodan nodded.

'That's a good point. I'll keep it in mind.' He smiled.

'Still, it does state a value,' he said softly, as if talking to himself. 'We can achieve a transition, we can modulate hyperwaves and broadcast them. But we're at a loss as how to handle a being whose abode is in higher space. Anybody living in space of *n* dimensions eludes by this fact alone the grasp of those in (*n*-one) dimensional space.'

Khrest finally got up.

'So you realize that it's more sensible to abandon this expedition?'

Rhodan swivelled around.

'No,' he said sternly. 'I can't see that at all. I doubt very much that it's more sensible, as you say.'

Rhodan leaned against the backrest of his chair and stretched out his hand.

'It's still the same old problem, Khrest,' he said. 'We encounter something new. It arouses our curiosity and we try to find out more about the new discovery. There are only two reasons which will force us to give up. Either we'll eventually learn all we want to know or the venture begins to endanger our lives, or has already taken our lives.

'Neither one of these cases has occurred. Therefore, we'll keep trying to satisfy our curiosity.'

Khrest gave no answer.

'Have you been able to decipher the notations of the structure sensor?' asked Rhodan.

'No. I don't think it can be done.'

'Aren't you a little too hasty in your assumption?'

Khrest shrugged his shoulders.

'The structure sensor is an instrument which enables us to observe warping of the space continuum, the four-dimensional space, mind you. The effect itself though is of a higher dimension which explains the fast propagation velocity.

'Nobody has ever thought about modulating such an effect – as evidently was done here – and, accordingly, the structure sensor wasn't built to be a receiver. You can't receive radar signals with a stovepipe, to give a good example.'

'Yes, you can,' protested Rhodan. 'All you have to do is to prepare the stovepipe for the purpose.'

Khrest looked surprised.

'Are you seriously implying that the structure sensor . . .'

'I'm quite serious,' replied Rhodan. 'Indeed, that's what I'm going to do. However, it will be necessary to work out many equations. Do you want to help me with it?'

'Heaven protect mankind's mathematics!' laughed Rhodan cheerfully. 'Arkonide math is so advanced that it's defined hyper-oscillation with such a simple expression that it can't be broken down any further. By contrast, Terrestrial math does it the hard way to explain this occurrence. First one has to derive the formula and, in the process, one gets the idea how to apply it in a higher degree.'

Khrest nodded agreeably but a little derisively.

'I wish I knew what you meant.'

'What is a hyper-oscillation?' asked Rhodan. 'Let's be careful. It's produced by variable, periodic gravitational reaction. We can create such a variable gravitational reaction if we use a micro-accelerator to bombard high-energy protons in certain intervals so that their energy produces new particles.'

He leaned over the table on which he had spread out his computations.

'You know the formalism of your mathematics which defines a particle and converts it into an antiparticle simply by rotating the hyper-complex system of co-ordinates?'

Khrest nodded. He began to get the idea and it left him speechless.

'Good. Then you know that I have only to couple the conventional micro-accelerator with a similar accelerator for antiparticles to ...'

Khrest waved his hand.

'Wait a minute!' he exclaimed. 'And don't always say "only". If you can prove your theory in practice you'll have revolutionized the entire science of physics.'

Rhodan nodded casually.

'Maybe so. All I know so far is that in order to obtain sufficient antiparticles I'll need so much energy that I'll have to disconnect our protective screens temporarily.'

Nevertheless, he took the chance. Time was of the essence. The structure sensor kept repeating the same program in regular intervals.

But how long would it be before the patience of the unknown was exhausted? Until now he had always stressed that his candidates should not spend any more time than assigned for the solution of a problem.

How much time was allotted now?

Rhodan constructed the micro-accelerator for antiparticles. He required two days – Terrestrial time – for it.

During those two days the technical surveillance registered four times that one or the other of the generators for the protective screen was running dry. This effect never lasted more than ten seconds and, being prepared for the situation, they prevented the *Stardust* from suffering any damage.

Each time after such a period of idling, however, the spot of light which – as Rhodan believed – came from a higher universe, showed up on the observation screen.

On the third day after the start of the project Rhodan wanted to produce his antiparticles. The micro-accelerator which the hyper-transmitter used, as it were, for an oscillation track served simultaneously as a reservoir. Protons injected into a circular track were kept on the same level for years.

In theory Rhodan would only once need a current of antiparticles to keep his new accelerator operating for years. However, since antiparticles had a great tendency to combine with normal particles and get lost by radiating away their mass, he would have to 'recharge' the anti-accelerator frequently.

'Will it do us any good?' muttered Rhodan, reflecting on the experiment.

For nearly an hour *Stardust II* was deprived of any protective screen except the one which gravity neutralizers produced. The output was reduced and the ship secured a firmer hold by sinking about one hundred and fifty feet into the soft ground.

None the less, the procedure was critical. The gigantic body of the vessel presented an expansive surface for the attacks of the storm. Rhodan had ordered all men of the crew to their stations and had given instructions that this experiment should be interrupted any time the ship was in serious danger.

Then he waited.

It was an unpleasant suspense. The *Stardust*, stripped of its protective screen was too big to be unaffected by the storm, was tossed around like a steamer in a hurricane.

But the hour passed without any serious damage to the vessel. Only one valuable instrument broke because it had not been secured to its base, disregarding Rhodan's instructions to the contrary.

The second micro-accelerator was in operating condition. Rhodan and Khrest installed it in the structure sensor and knew that the new oscillation track coupled with the old one was capable of receiving circular, polarized gravity radiation as well as transmitting it. They had thereby boosted the effectiveness of the operation one dimension higher.

'What time is the next transmission due?' asked Rhodan.

Bell looked at the clock.

'In fourteen minutes.'

Rhodan sank into a chair and waited.

'Two more minutes,' said Bell.

Rhodan got up and went to the structure sensor. He smiled oddly at Khrest.

'You can laugh all you want if it doesn't work,' Rhodan said.

'One minute to go,' interrupted Bell impatiently.

The hatch rolled open and Thora came in. Without uttering a word she sat down beside Khrest and waited, too.

'It should come now,' declared Rhodan.

And come it did.

A point of light flashed on the screen of the oscillograph, wandered around and, for a fraction of a second, gave the impression of getting lost in the meaningless pattern which it had already drawn a hundred times.

But then, as though it had changed its intentions, it began to form a sine wave and ran across the screen. It flickered once, twice and then it stopped. The modulation was clearly visible in the fine, uneven nodules of the curve.

The sixteen seconds had passed in a flash. The screen went dark. Rhodan stared at it as if he did not believe his eyes. Khrest got up shakily and turned to Rhodan.

'I'm not one to bandy around fancy words,' he said earnestly, 'but . . .'

'Later,' Rhodan interrupted almost rudely. It frightened Khrest to see how suddenly Rhodan's activity developed with renewed, explosive force.

'Bell! Ask Tanaka Seiko to come here immediately. Khrest, please help me. We want to play this transcript for Tanaka.'

The structure sensor was switched over. Tanaka came in and watched in astonishment. Rhodan was feeding the tape just now recorded back into the structure sensor and induced it to transmit again what it had received earlier.

'Listen, Tanaka!' Rhodan demanded. 'Tell me if you can hear anything!'

He turned the set on. There could be no doubt for even a second that Tanaka was receiving something. He leaned forward in his characteristic, rigid posture and gave the impression of falling out of his chair at any moment.

After sixteen seconds had passed, he remained motionless for a while. A few minutes later he sank back in his chair, took a deep breath and looked around with amazement.

'I understood it very clearly, sir,' he said finally. 'Never before has it been so easy to decipher a message as this one.'

'What did it say?'

'"Even though you have perceived this, you must follow the way to the mountain. Only there is the light hidden. Do not wait long. The mighty ones of" – here follows a name, sir. As you know, I can't receive names but I know it meant the planet on which we are, namely – "the mighty ones of Gol will overpower you if you hesitate too long. Do not come without the higher knowledge!"'

'Is that all?'

'Yes, sir, that was all.'

'Thank you, Tanaka; you may leave.'

CHAPTER FOUR

THE VALLEY OF THE PHANTOMS

'If one considers that this message was being beamed for quite a number of days already, one is led to believe that we should hurry up,' said Rhodan gravely.

Khrest shook his head.

'Speaking frankly, it makes me feel very uncomfortable. What for instance, does it mean: "The mighty ones of Gol will overpower you if you hesitate too long".'

Rhodan shrugged his shoulders.

'I have no idea. We'll find out, though.'

'And what is the higher knowledge?' asked Thora.

'We tried to guess this once before, didn't we? It could be that he's referring to parapsychological powers, as we call it.'

Rhodan had three of the caterpillars at his disposal such as he had used on his first trip. He did not hesitate to employ all three of them simultaneously.

He chose not to install any additional protective screen generators since they would have taken up even more room than the gravitation neutralizers. Instead he insisted that each vehicle be armed. Therefore, each vehicle was provided with a medium-heavy disintegrator, a neutron beamer and the usual thermo-impulse weapons. Furthermore, a movable catapult was mounted in each of the vehicles. At first nobody knew what purpose they were to serve.

Twenty containers with heavy-gauge metal walls were loaded into each vehicle, apparently to be used with the catapults. The technician stated that they contained liquid oxygen and ignition fuses and from then on everybody was aware of their application.

Oxygen and methane mixed in the right proportions formed an explosive combination. Anybody forced to defend himself against a foe on a methane planet could not do anything cheaper than inject an adequate portion of oxygen into the atmosphere and ignite the mixture at the right moment.

Composition of the crew presented a problem. Rhodan decided, contrary to his previous objections, to give the command of the second carrier to Bell. As far as the third one was concerned, he had a very definite notion. Although he was commander of the *Stardust* he preferred in this case not to give an order but to express his wish.

He addressed Khrest: 'I'd like to ask you if you could overcome your reluctance to take part in this expedition and assume command of the third vehicle.'

Khrest looked astonished. He twisted his face into a sad smile.

'Thank you for your tactfulness, Rhodan,' he answered. 'You meant to say fear instead of reluctance, didn't you? Well, I'll come along.'

Khrest clapped his hands in human fashion and exclaimed: 'Of all people you had to pick the most harmless Arkonide to prove to your men that Arkonides are not completely worthless.'

They both laughed.

'Each vehicle will be occupied by two mutants and one officer,' declared Rhodan. 'I'll give you Tama Yokida, the telekinetic mutant; Ishy Matsu, the telepath; and Captain Klein.'

Bell drove with Betty Toufry, Ralf Marten and Major Nyssen.

Rhodan had his old crew and, in addition, the telekinetic Anne Sloane.

Thora took over command of the *Stardust*.

After Rhodan's antiparticle experiment *Stardust II* had been raised again and returned to its normal position. The three vehicles left the bottom lock without any trouble and made their way through the now somewhat shallower methane lake towards the southern shore.

The communication between the three vehicles, and with the vessel as well, functioned perfectly. At least the start of the expedition was under a good omen and Rhodan thanked his lucky star.

The troubles began in front of the mountain wall where the infrared searchlight had given up its ghost on Rhodan's first trip.

Rhodan's vehicle was first in line. Rhodan had no intention of circumventing the barrier in a great detour. The terrain was treacherous and each additional yard meant more danger.

Deringhouse was stationed at the catapult.

'Bomb ready for ejection!'

Rhodan warned the other vehicles.

'Ready! Fire!'

The cannister was visible in the cone of the searchlight, wobbling awkwardly as it was hurled from the catapult. It was still inside the gravity neutralization field and followed the same trajectory as it would have done on Earth.

Rhodan had increased the enegry of the field and extended it close to the mountain barrier. The canister descended in free flight towards the ground and passed through the rim of the field.

It looked as if somebody had stopped it in mid-flight. It dropped to the ground too quickly for the eyes to follow and burst under the tremendous force of the impact. Tiny droplets of oxygen mixed with the methane of the atmosphere and as Rhodan ignited it the observation screen was filled by a single, painfully bright stroke of lightning.

There was a powerful pressure wave which shook up the vehicle.

The bomb had torn a hole in the wall; there was no doubt about it. A deep crack ran from the ground to the ridge of the massive mountain wall.

But, on the other hand, there was also no doubt that the crack was too narrow for the vehicles.

'Second bomb!' ordered Rhodan.

Deringhouse shoved the second canister into the catapult.

Rhodan took the mike.

'Attention! We're going to blast it a second time!'

Deringhouse signalled with a nod.

'Fire!'

The canister took off shakily, rose to the apex and descended again to the outer limits of the field.

'Look there, sir!' shouted Deringhouse.

Rhodan saw it, too.

A small, glowing sphere floated at the bottom of the mountain wall, just above where the canister was going to hit after leaving the field.

Rhodan watched the canister pass the border of the field and drop suddenly. He narrowed his eyes in expectation of the glaring explosion which had to follow. But nothing happened!

There was some kind of will-o'-the-wisp, not the slightest trace of destruction in the mountain. Flickering, a white light spread out – a slowly burning fire!

It did not go out. It formed a sphere with about a fifteen foot diameter which glittered and floated in front of the wall.

'The small sphere is gone, sir,' reported Deringhouse breathlessly.

The diameter of the small sphere had measured no more than twenty inches.

Rhodan shook his head. 'No,' he replied. 'There it is!'

He pointed to the fifteen foot sphere.

Deringhouse stared at him, unbelieving.

'But that's impossible, sir!'

'No time for discussions. Get the disintegrator!'

Deringhouse turned the heavy weapon around.

'Fire at the wall!' ordered Rhodan. 'But shoot to miss the sphere!'

Deringhouse obeyed.

After ten seconds of shooting the crack in the wall was wide enough to let at least two cars go through side by side. Deringhouse, moving mechanically, turned back the disintegrator to its rest position. He stared with big frightened eyes at the glittering ball which performed some kind of a dance in front of the wall about thirty feet to the right of the opening.

'Forward at top speed!' barked Rhodan into the telecom. 'Khrest, come alongside. The gap isn't big enough for two cars. Bell, watch the sphere but don't try any experiments!'

Khrest reacted with satisfactory speed. Side by side the two vehicles spurted forward, reached the gap and disappeared inside. Bell followed closely.

Rhodan breathed a sigh of relief when he saw that the disintegrator had penetrated the full depth of the wall.

The sight beyond the mountain barrier was encouraging. A fairly smooth plain stretched before the caterpillar as far as the searchlight reached. There were hills to the left and right and steep mountain peaks rose high up into the sky in the background. But the high valley in between was so wide that an entire company of vehicles could drive abreast through it in comfort.

Bell's car was the last to leave the gap, and in a hurry, Rhodan swept the terrain with the searchlight. There was nothing to be seen except the other two vehicles and the rocky desolation of Gol. No hint of any danger whatsoever.

'All right,' growled Rhodan with satisfaction. 'Let's go!'

According to the reports from the range finder the mountain for which they searched was at a distance of one hundred and thirty miles from the ship. Considering that this was measured in a straight line and that the vehicles were not always able to proceed directly, they could assume with sufficient accuracy that it would take at least eight hours to reach the mountain.

Eight hours in the neighbourhood of glowing balls which loved, so to speak, powerful methane-oxygen explosions like dessert and used the energy from these explosions to increase their volume.

Khrest semed to ponder the same thought.

'Did you observe the sphere?' he inquired from his vehicle.

'Of course,' answered Rhodan.

'What do you think of it?'

'Very simple. The first explosion had lured it. When it came, it had a diameter of perhaps twenty inches and, evidently, a ravenous appetite.'

'An appetite?'

'Yes. It put itself exactly in the flight curve of the second oxygen canister and *devoured* the energy of the explosion. It seemed to veritably thrive on the diet since it grew suddenly to a tenfold diameter.'

'Do you really believe that this is what happened?' asked Khrest skeptically.

'I don't believe it,' Rhodan replied. 'I've seen it!'

Deringhouse tapped Rhodan on the shoulder.

'I don't know if I should bother you with it, sir,' said Deringhouse cautiously and pointed to the observation screen, 'but the ball is here again.'

From then on, it never left them. It jumped up and down behind the vehicles and lost about twenty per cent of its volume within three hours.

It was a weird and mysterious apparition.

'I can't help it,' remarked Bell as the three vehicles rounded a curve on the steep slope of the mountain.

'This thing makes me nervous. Can't we do something about it?'

'What would you suggest?' asked Rhodan.

'Shoot at it, for example.'

To the surprise of everybody who listened in on the conversation, Rhodan said quietly: 'Okay. Column halt. Commander Bell will try his luck.'

The vehicles stopped with motors running, and they all watched the movement on top of the last car as Bell swung his weapon around.

Bell's voice could be heard. 'Ready, Nyssen?'

'Ready.'

The mighty beam from the powerful weapon could be clearly seen from Rhodan's vehicle.

Nyssen's shot hit the sphere dead centre. Even on the infrared observation screen, which normally showed only black and white, it was obvious that the sphere changed colours. Bell took this to mean success of his action and shouted triumphantly.

But then he gulped. The ball, far from being impressed by the disintegrator's impact, began to swell. It had regained its original colour and grew rapidly.

The eyes of the people in the carriers were riveted to the visiscreens.

Bell's groaning came distinctly over the telecom. Everybody seemed to be speechless.

Rhodan was the only one who had foreseen this result.

'Forward!' ordered Rhodan curtly. 'Nobody will pay any more attention to that thing. It's not hurting us and there is, therefore, no reason to let it worry us.'

His command made them all snap out of their brooding.

Tanaka Seiko complained about a headache.

'Since when?' inquired Rhodan.

'Since the shot,' answered Tanaka, moaning.

Rhodan nodded. The sphere emitted hyper-radiation which either partially or in all its phases affected Tanaka's brain. Since the sphere had soaked up the total energy of the disintegrator shot its radiation evidently had become strong enough to cause the Japanese a headache. This was obvious and in no sense puzzling.

What Rhodan found interesting, however, was that Tanaka on his first trip had almost fainted under the effect of the radiation from a much smaller ball. There seemed to be, therefore, at least two types of such balls and they differed from each other in their energy – or the dimension – of their radiation emission.

The vehicles started their advance again and neared the end of the upper valley which had allowed them so unexpectedly to proceed quickly and without obstacles.

At the end of the valley the big effort began which diverted their attention from the glowing sphere for hours. Rhodan had to make a choice between a detour which would take them far afield and cost them at least twenty additional hours or climb up extremely steep slopes which the vehicles might not be able to manage. He had no way of knowing this beforehand.

In spite of this uncertainty he decided to do the latter, largely also because he had, just before making his decision, received Thora's message from the *Stardust*:

'Five of our protective screen generators failed for almost ten minutes. At the moment we are observing numerous bodies of light moving around in the vicinity of the ship.'

Her concern about the ship could be heard in her voice. Rhodan had requested her to keep him informed about any change in the situation. He had no doubt any more that it was possible for these energy bodies to soak up the energy of the protective screen and thereby to exhaust the generators.

He kept his three vehicles close together and started to climb. The wall which towered before them was too high, and the searchlight could not reach up to the ridge. Rhodan believed, however, that – judging from the angle formed between two adjacent mountain slopes – it was safe to conclude that the obstacle did not exceed a height of forty-five hundred feet.

The crew aboard the carriers had mixed feelings. Tanaka Seiko was still suffering from a splitting headache because the huge sphere kept following the vehicle doggedly. Rhodan had retreated into the cold and determined toughness which was at the core of his personality in such critical situations. Reginald Bell and Major Deringhouse vied with him in this toughness but embellished it with a certain show of flippancy and a devil-may-care attitude. Khrest had not uttered a word in the last few hours. He seemed convinced that they were on a straight path to hell and so apparently was Anne Sloane, who was squatting apathetically on the floor of Rhodan's car with a vacant look and showing little interest.

Major Nyssen was a strange man. Rhodan had never known this aspect of his qualities. Nyssen, who outwardly so much resembled Reginald Bell, had developed during the last few hours a certain fanatical urge – without losing his sense of reality or overestimating the limiting circumstances of this expedition – to subdue the energy bodies which seemed to constitute the greatest danger to the *Stardust*, not expecting those threatening from the adverse atmospherical and gravitational conditions of Gol.

Nyssen was conducting regular discussions with Rhodan over the telecom and his résumé was as follows:

'We won't be able to control them with our heavy weapons, sir. They eat energy as people eat cake. We'll have to invent something entirely new or find a form of energy which is detrimental to them.'

Rhodan agreed with him.

'A pass, sir!' shouted Deringhouse enthusiastically all of a sudden. 'A pass!'

During the last two hours the vehicles had climbed about twenty-four hundred feet. The crossing had been very difficult. There was nothing one could call a road by any stretch of the imagination.

But here, at a height of twenty-four hundred feet, a pass appeared in the form of a narrow crevice which penetrated the mountain wall almost exactly in a southern direction. It was heaven sent, they thought. Rhodan rushed in with his vehicle. Khrest followed him – endeavouring anxiously not to fall behind more than fifty or seventy-five feet – with Bell at the tail end, remarking:

'Now I'd like to see whether that one hundred and fifty foot monster will squeeze through behind us!'

He was referring to the energy sphere and if he believed that the bottleneck would prevent the sphere from pursuing them, he was very quickly disillusioned.

The sphere stretched out into a form which could not yet even be described in geometric terms. In any case, it was more than five hundred feet high and very thin and slender. In this fashion the former sphere danced through the pass like a will-o'-the-wisp.

After a few hundred yards in a straight course the pass began to wind. Rhodan reduced his speed and followed the sharp curves, worrying all the time that the pass might become so narrow as to make it impossible for them to go on. In that case they would have to return backward since the crevice left no room for turning around.

However, nothing of the sort happened. The fissure continued at a constant width through the mountain. Then it ended unexpectedly out in the open at the south wall on an almost vertical precipice.

Rhodan stopped the vehicle. He rotated the searchlight and studied the picture on the observation screen.

'Nothing!' grumbled Deringhouse, who was looking over Rhodan's shoulder. 'But we can move another six feet forward, sir.'

Rhodan nodded. He cautiously pulled the car up and the front end moved out of the gap's opening.

The field of sight was immediately widened.

The first thing Rhodan saw was a rocky ledge which was leading from the exit of the pass, descending slightly along the mountain wall from east to west. If he steered carefully he would be able to turn the vehicle onto the ledge and drive down.

Down? Where to?

Rhodan pointed the searchlight towards the south. He painted a white beam of light in the darkness as far as the powerful searchlight could reach without revealing any details of the terrain.

'A valley basin,' said Rhodan, 'too deep to recognize anything from up here.'

'Would you mind switching off the searchlight for a

minute, sir?' asked Deringhouse.

Rhodan looked at him puzzledly.

'Of course not. What's the mystery?'

He turned off the searchlight.

A second later, after the intensive infrared light had disappeared from the screen, Rhodan saw what Deringhouse was after.

A vast multitude of pale and eerie glowing forms were now populating the observation screen. Bodies of light, numbering in the thousands and in at least that many different shapes. Only Deringhouse's sharp eyes were able to make them out in the brightness of the searchlight.

'The Valley of the Phantoms!' murmured Deringhouse.

His voice was derisive, but not derisive enough to hide the fact of how much he was distressed by the impression.

'What's the matter?' came Bell's voice from the last vehicle. 'Why don't we go on? Where's the Valley of the Phantoms?'

'Right here!' answered Rhodan. 'Directly in front of us. Watch out when you turn around at the spot where my car is standing now. Let's go on!'

The ledge turned out to be a very suitable road for the cars, as though somebody who knew they were coming on an expedition had laid it out for them and their three vehicles.

While driving on the ledge Rhodan used his searchlights to illuminate the way ahead and lost sight of the wavering, glowing bodies. But he had not forgotten about them. The big question was whether the peculiar phenomena would remain as peaceful when the three lonely vehicles encountered them in such overwhelming numbers as the one that was dancing behind them in its hypergeometric shape.

The mountain wall curved around. The direction became southeast for a while and turned again exactly south. According to Rhodan's calculations the mountain peak which was their goal could be no farther than fifty miles away.

When the ledge had descended the twenty-four hundred feet which they had climbed up on the other side of the mountain, it became wider and finally merged into the level floor of the valley.

Rhodan stopped his vehicle as soon as he was far enough ahead to allow the other two vehicles to get off the ledge.

He turned his searchlight off again. But the lights from the other vehicles threw off too much glare. He asked Khrest and Bell to switch them off too, which they did.

And then they saw on all three observation screens a strange and awesome picture.

The huge valley was filled with bodies of light. There was a whole army of them.

They formed a front about twelve hundred feet south of the three vehicles.

The basin before them was the only way they could proceed farther south. Rhodan was convinced that the mountain bordering the basin in the south was the one for which they were looking.

The vehicles had to push through between the glowing bodies. So far they had not proved to be hostile except in the case where they latched onto the protective screen of *Stardust II*. But until now they had appeared only alone or in small quantities. There was no way of predicting how thousands of them would behave.

Rhodan conferred for some time with the drivers of the other two vehicles.

Bell's answer was straightforward: 'We've got to break through! The sooner the better.'

Khrest made his decision and told Rhodan: 'I leave it to you, Rhodan. I'll follow your instructions.'

Rhodan decided to break through. However, he attempted to set up some rear guard for his expedition. Since Tanaka was out of action because of his headache, he told Deringhouse to call the *Stardust* and give Thora a report about their situation.

Deringhouse gave the call signal and waited for response. But he got no answer. He tried again but had no more luck than before.

Rhodan contacted the other two vehicles. They had received Deringhouse's call correctly.

There was nothing wrong with the transmitter.

But the *Stardust* did not reply!

CHAPTER FIVE

ENCOUNTER WITH THE GHOSTS

Thora had watched the vehicles ascending the northern mountain slope and going through the pass as best she could with the imperfect communication setup. None but the most vital equipment had been installed in the vehicles. Communication by television, for instance, had been considered superfluous and was, therefore, eliminated. Every square inch of space and each ounce of weight had been utilized. Rhodan had regarded it an unnecessary luxury to look into each other's eyes while talking together.

Thora held her breath when Rhodan drove out to the narrow ledge and she became very jittery when Khrest followed him. She breathed a deep sigh of relief when the pass opened up before the vehicles and the perilous ride came to an end.

She vicariously shared the trip through the pass while listening to Reginald Bell's remarks and heard Deringhouse mention the Valley of the Phantoms.

That was the last she heard. The next moment things began to happen to the *Stardust* which made them think that the world had come to an end for them, had it not been for a last saving grace.

Thora was so engrossed in the telecom conversation between the three vehicles that she was unable to determine immediately upon hearing the first howling of the alarm sirens which sector of the ship had been endangered. She jumped up, regarded the control panel with frightened eyes and felt panic rising up in her when she could not find the emergency signal.

'All neutralizing machines running idle!' shouted a voice from the telecom above the din of the sirens.

The engineer sounded irritated and impatient. He was used to Rhodan's lightning fast reactions, not to the slow and panicky functioning of an Arkonide brain.

'What can we do?' Thora inquired hastily.

Then she remembered that the man did not understand her language. She repeated her question in English.

'That's what I wanted you to tell me!' screamed the engineer, who was so distraught over the failure of the generators that he neglected to show the customary respect.

'What's the matter with the protective screen?'

'It's still intact. The gravity neutralization field is completely gone; but I can hold the ship with the engines.'

The sirens had stopped howling. Some of Thora's tension subsided as silence returned.

'Keep holding the ship!' Thora ordered. 'I'll try to find out what's going on out there.'

The engineer signed off and Thora called the range finder officer.

'Can you see anything?'

'No. The observation screen turned completely black.'

Thora switched on the big all-around screen in the Control Centre. Whereas it had before shown a homogenous grey, now it showed an equally homogenous deep black void.

The Arkonide woman went hastily to the receiver where she had heard the conversations between the three vehicles only a few minutes ago. She had not turned it off. But it was dead and did not even make the usual slight background noise.

Thora began to understand that something was happening which she had never before experienced. She wished Perry Rhodan were back to give her some advicc and she cursed him at the same time because he had dared to leave her alone with the giant ship in this monstrous world.

Somebody has got to get out there, was her first thought. *We have to find out what's going on outside.*

Her second thought was that nobody would be willing to venture out and she could not blame anyone.

What did Rhodan always say? Don't ask questions – give orders!

How easy it would have been for her a few years ago when she first met human beings and considered them a race of foolish savages! But now?

The telecom clicked.

'It's swarming with lights out there, ma'am.'

The face of Wuriu Sengu, the 'seer', appeared on the small visiscreen.

Thora nodded.

She recalled the experience Reginald Bell had a few hours earlier, bombarding these phantoms with his disintegrator. There were a number of different weapons at hand on the *Stardust*. Perhaps one of them would be useful.

'Come to the Command Centre, Sengu!' Thora ordered the Japanese.

Sengu nodded and disconnected the line.

Thora instructed the Weapon Control Section to get ready to fire the impulse beamer and neutron missiles. The all clear came as Sengu entered the Command Centre.

'You can easily trace the trajectory of a thermo-impulse beamer,' Thora advised Sengu. 'The battle station will open fire in a few seconds. I'd like to know what effect it will have.'

Wuriu took his position. He stared at a spot he had selected on the wall of the room. Somebody who did not know him, and was not aware that the Japanese had the faculty to influence the crystalline structure of matters by the strength of his will alone so that it became transparent for him, would have thought that he was pondering a serious problem.

'Fire!' commanded Thora.

She watched Sengu.

He kept staring at the wall for several minutes. Thora saw his forehead break out in a sweat. She wanted to query him but she knew it was useless to interrupt his concentrated attention.

Suddenly he slumped forward.

'Stop it!' he gasped. 'At once!'

'Hold fire!' Thora responded.

Sengu flung himself on a chair. He was breathing so hard and fast that it took a while until he could utter a word.

'They swallow ... everything. The thermo-rays are piercing their bodies but don't go through. The glowing becomes more intensive and they're growing in size. It looks as though they're consuming the energy of the shots.'

Sengu was unaware that Thora knew about the similar experiment Bell had conducted a few hours ago.

She was thinking about making a second attempt with the neutron missiles. Neutrons were corpuscles, not energy in the sense of . . .

'Watch out!' shouted Sengu. 'They're coming!'

Thora felt miserable and helpless.

'What are they doing?' she asked breathlessly.

One more moment and she knew.

A mighty jolt shook the ship. Thora fell to the floor and when she tried to get up again after the initial shock she felt that her weight had increased threefold.

Sengu sank deeper in the chair and kept looking through the wall.

'They're real close now,' he panted. 'They're sitting on the outer hull.'

A voice shouted from the telecom:

'Engine power down to seventy per cent. Strength of neutralization field on board greatly reduced.'

It was the engineer again and this time his voice sounded more frightened than impatient.

Thora struggled to get up and dragged herself to the mike.

'Try to start!' she breathed.

It was as if the gravity had forced her body into a tight straitjacket. It was difficult for her to breathe.

'If you take the responsibility, ma'am!' answered the engineer.

Lights began to flicker all over the control panel as the engineer took over the steering of the ship in the technical department. Thora watched the lights as if she had never seen them before and waited for the reassuring green of the starting signal.

Finally it came. One second, two seconds, three seconds – it was shining brightly on the panel. Then it went out and the ship had not moved.

Thora moaned inarticulately, shaken by fear.

'We've lost all power!' reported the engineer. The realization of his inability to do anything about it had apparently restored his calm.

Wuriu Sengu uttered a muffled groan.

'They've become gigantic, gigantic . . .'

'But we have to do something!' cried Thora.

She took a step towards Sengu.

Something happened at this moment. She was pulled forward and tumbled to the floor for the second time within a few minutes.

She had fallen very hard and was dizzy. Lifting herself up, she glanced at Sengu. She felt no more pain when she turned her neck. Thora rose and noticed that the heavy weight had lifted from her and her body felt normal again.

The Japanese smiled.

'They're gone,' he said quietly. 'They vanished all of a sudden.'

Thora looked around as if trying to find the reason for this miracle in the Command Centre.

Her gaze lingered on the oscillograph screen of the structure sensor. It showed the brightly shining, modulated sine waves of the message from the unknown being for whose sake Rhodan had risked this daring journey.

She looked mechanically at the clock.

The transmission was on time as usual.

Rhodan had just made up his mind to abandon the expedition and return to the *Stardust* when the vessel contacted him again. He had started the car and was about to steer it back in a loop when Deringhouse yelled behind him:

'They're back again, sir!'

'Calling Rhodan. *Stardust* calling Commander Rhodan!' sounded the telecom.

It was Thora. Rhodan could not remember when her voice sounded so meek. Impatiently he grabbed the microphone.

'Rhodan speaking. What was the matter with you?'

The noise which preceded her answer could have been a sigh of relief or an atmospheric disturbance.

'We were attacked,' Thora said, then gave a somewhat confused but detailed report of the events during the preceding minutes.

Rhodan interrupted her when he had understood her story.

'Can you start?' he asked.

'Yes, we can now.'

'Take off and stay at a safe altitude, let's say a thousand miles up, until you get my next message. I don't believe that these lights venture out that far.'

'All right. But what's the purpose?'

'We've come here to a valley and as soon as we can find out what kind of company these assembled phantoms make I want you to land the *Stardust* in this basin. I'll give you the co-ordinates.'

Thora seemed depressed but Rhodan paid no attention.

'Keep in touch with us at all times,' he advised her.

Rhodan had his own ideas about the incident to which the *Stardust* had almost fallen victim by a hairbreadth. There was no reasonable explanation as to why the light bodies had suddenly retreated from the ship, unless there was a connection between their retreat and the simultaneous arrival of the unknown's message.

Was there a possible relationship? Was the form of energy which the unknown used to send his messages the same that Major Nyssen had tried to discover for hours?

Khrest called.

'Rhodan, do you really want to go through under these circumstances?'

'You bet I do,' Rhodan assured him. 'We've practically no protective field around us, nothing therefore to whet the appetite of these lights.'

He trusted that no one called his bluff. The glowing bodies had even swallowed the low energy of the infrared searchlight beam and one could expect that they would be very much interested in the powerful gravity neutralization field.

But Rhodan had an inspiration.

'Column, forward!' he ordered sharply.

His vehicle was again leading the pack. They approached almost leisurely the front of the lights which were dancing around by the thousands in the dark valley.

Rhodan switched off the searchlight. He could find his way by the light of the luminous bodies.

'What's the ball behind us doing?' he asked Bell.

'It keeps on doing the same thing all the time,' answered Bell. 'Dancing and rocking.'

'You didn't notice anything different?'

'No.'

Then the vehicles reached the forefront of the luminous bodies and from that moment on Rhodan had no time to think about any problems other than those which he was presently facing.

At first the lights took no notice of the vehicles. They were separated far enough so that the heavy vehicles could easily pass through between them.

'What do you know!' exclaimed Bell, surprised 'They're not so bad after all.'

Rhodan rotated the antenna of the optical screen. In the meantime they had advanced so deeply inside the front that they could no longer see any open terrain. Before them, at their sides and behind them, everywhere the lighted veils of the incredible energy bodies were swaying.

Rhodan gnashed his teeth.

He looked at his watch. Ten minutes had passed.

He knew that his luck was bound to run out and that he could not drive through this mass much longer without getting into trouble. The end had to come sometime; but when?

Fifteen minutes.

'Can you see the end of it?' asked Bell.

'No, not yet.'

After twenty minutes the view in front of the vehicles still looked the same as when they had passed through the first row of the glowing ghosts.

The basin stretched wide and far in all directions and the entire valley floor seemed to be occupied by the luminous bodies.

Rhodan asked himself why the phantoms had specifically chosen this place to assemble and none other. Was something here which attracted them particularly? Or could they have – like other intelligent beings – developed certain habits so that they always met in the same location?

Twenty-five minutes.

Rhodan had not driven very fast. Even more important than passing through this swarm of glowing veils and shreds was an experiment which he wanted to conduct. He intended to try it first of all and jeopardize his men by this experiment.

Thirty minutes.

Since the beginning of the experiment the vehicles had travelled about twelve miles. They could have driven much faster on the fairly smooth ground.

It started in the thirty-second minute.

Rhodan noticed, to begin with, that the luminous veils were not standing as far apart as before. He had to turn the steering wheel very hard to pass between them without colliding.

'All weapons ready to fire!' ordered Rhodan.

He could hear Khrest gasping for air.

'What do you want to shoot? Not these energy bodies?'

'You'll see. Everybody, please listen: we'll concentrate the fire from all our weapons – except the oxygen canisters for the time being – on a point even with Khrest's vehicle and six hundred feet west of the line of our column.

'I'll give the order to fire. Nobody shoots ahead of time.'

He did not mean to act very mysteriously but there was

no more time for long speeches. The lights had almost closed ranks and Rhodan could picture what was going to happen in a few moments.

Tanaka Seiko fainted. His mind could no longer withstand the strain.

Rhodan had no choice left. The front before him was closed and if he wanted to drive on he had to go through the curtain of light which the phantoms formed ahead of them.

He did not hesitate. He was of the opinion that the real substance of the energy bodies existed in hyper-space and that the light emanated from them would not harm the vehicles by itself.

'Anne, operate the generators!'

Rhodan had to repeat his command in order to make her snap out of her brooding.

'Don't be afraid, baby!' he smiled when he saw how pale her face was.

Then it happened.

There was a jerk and the vehicle stopped. Not because the vehicle was blocked by something but because the engine no longer had enough power to move the car.

'Anne, give it more!' panted Rhodan.

He had thought that the effect would be somewhat weaker. He knew that the light bodies had begun to satisfy their appetites with the neutralizing field of the vehicles.

They did it with surprising voracity. From one second to the next the gravity inside the vehicle grew to dizzying values.

Nine G's in his estimation.

He thought of Khrest and his Arkonide body that was

no longer able to cope with the strain.

His hand, heavy as lead, reached for the microphone and he called: 'Fire all guns!'

Deringhouse pulled the levers. The mighty high energy beam of the disintegrator cannon made the body of the car vibrate for a few seconds. The neutron ray gun went off with a singing sound and the thermo-impulse weapon completed the concert with a deep, muffled droning.

Rhodan saw on the observation screen that the other vehicles had reacted just as quickly. Glittering energy rays cut through the multitude of dancing lights and crossed at the target point in the distance.

The effect which Rhodan had anticipated, however, did not take place for a while.

It seemed an endless time that the pressure, which made breathing very difficult, held the occupants of the vehicle captive. Actually, it lasted only a few minutes as Rhodan watched the clock.

Then the pressure began to diminish.

At the same time the hitherto closed front of the luminous bodies before Rhodan's car began to break up. For the first time a gap opened up and Rhodan could be heard shouting in undisguised triumph:

'Let's go on! Full speed ahead!'

The vehicles rumbled on. They had not yet regained their original weight. As yet a few of the phantoms had not recognized that some place else – six hundred feet to the west – there was much richer fare for their hunger than the weak neutralizing fields could offer.

But with every passing second the vehicle became lighter till it finally roared away at top speed. The light bodies concentrated at another spot. Even though the focal point of the combined weapons, the small expedition kept firing, moved as fast as the vehicles themselves, the lights – given the choice of two moving sources of energy – seemed to prefer to still their hunger with the stronger one.

Forty-one minutes after the three vehicles had ventured between the phantoms they reached the line at the other end. Suddenly it was dark and grey again before their eyes and Rhodan had to turn the antenna of the observation screen almost 180° around to get a glimpse of the light bodies.

'We got through!' Reginald Bell called jubilantly over the telecom.

Rhodan grinned hearing the wild joy in Bell's cry. The successful experiment filled him with a great sense of relief.

The luminous bodies were creations of a world of a higher order. Simply human beings – whose brains were so small that they were incapable of grasping fundamental four-dimensional problems and whose clumsy bodies emitted no other radiation than the infrared of their low body temperature – mere mortals had managed to outsmart these products of another world.

The light bodies made no attempt to pursue the vehicles. Rhodan instructed the other cars to continue the fire for the time being, but to shift the focus of the beams farther north.

The glowing shreds of veil gathered there, gorged themselves and kept growing. The weapons of the three vehicles expended a huge amount of energy, about ten thousand times more than the light bodies could have gained if they ravaged the neutralizing fields around the carriers.

The result could be noticed in their size. The more energy they swallowed the higher grew the front and the more intensive became their light.

The weapons kept shooting for fifteen more minutes. Then Rhodan ceased fire and waited.

The growth of the light bodies stopped abruptly. It was followed by a swirling movement of their masses as if they were seeking the full bowls of energy which had been so suddenly snatched from their hungry mouths.

But the vehicles were already too far away from them to detect the weak neutralizing fields. They continued dancing around for a few minutes and came to rest. They had had their feeding and had increased to twice their size.

Now they were finished!

Rhodan swung the antenna around.

'What does it look like ahead of us?' he asked.

The searchlight was switched on. As Rhodan was rotating it, the beam swept along a medium steep ledge rising up on the side of the mountain. The lower end of the ledge was no more than three hundred feet straight ahead.

Rhodan took a deep breath and all who heard him expected another command to spur them on for the impending nervous strain.

Instead Rhodan simply said: 'We are standing at *the mountain*!'

He emphasized the words so that everybody knew which mountain he meant.

CHAPTER SIX

A MESSAGE FROM THE UNKNOWN

After half an hour's search with their three powerful light beams it became clear to all of them that whatever there was to be found on this mountain it was not at the foot of the northern slope.

They agreed with Rhodan that the vehicles should drive up the mountain as far as they could go.

Rhodan was convinced that he would find what he was looking for at a higher altitude. He still firmly believed that the unknown being would give him another clue to the location he concealed or that it was really not at all hidden but something they could find if they kept their eyes open.

The north slope of the mighty mountain presented no difficulties for the vehicles.

Moreover, not only did the nebulous bodies in the valley remain peaceful but the sphere of light which had followed them for hours had abandoned its pursuit.

Approximately six thousand feet above the valley the mountain slope flattened out even more, until it eventually became a mesa of amazing proportions. Rhodan could rotate his searchlight wherever he wanted, reaching nothing but a void – proof that there was no solid object within a radius of over half a mile – no other solid matter except the level ground on which the vehicles stood.

Rhodan decided to stop for a rest.

He called the *Stardust.*

Thora answered immediately.

In the meantime the ship had, following his instructions, taken off from the ground and now hovered motionlessly at an altitude of twelve hundred miles.

Rhodan informed Thora about the events of the past hour and a half.

He concluded: 'We've learned two very important things – one's been made plausible and the other's been proved:

The energy bodies have only weakly developed capabilities to react to incidents taking place in three-dimensional space. They needed more than half an hour to notice that we were passing between them and that we had something to satisfy their hunger. Their sluggish reaction is what's been made plausible.

'But we've proved that they feed on energy. In any case, they've evidently no scruples and probably no appreciation of the damage they cause by their gluttony. They swallow whatever comes their way.

'I believe that – if one can apply this concept to such creatures – they really are *unintelligent* beings.

'Thora, I'd like to make another experiment if you don't mind?'

'What's that?' inquired Thora.

'Do you remember when the attack on the *Stardust* came to an end at the moment the unknown began to send his message and our structure sensor responded?'

'Yes, of course.'

'Okay. Connect the remodelled set to a powerful line. Raise the energy of the transmitter as high as it will go and bombard the light bodies with the radiation. I want to see how they react to it.'

The idea had never occurred to Thora, although it was really quite obvious.

'To do this, I will have to come down?' she asked, sulking a little and annoyed by her failure to see things in front of her nose.

'Certainly,' replied Rhodan seriously. 'If you charge the altered structure sensor to the limit it will have a range of at least three miles. You won't have to descend any lower than that. And something else!'

'Yes?'

'Flood the terrain up here with infrared light! We've rather poor visibility up here and not much of a view.'

Will I ever understand him? Thora asked herself.

What would she have done in Rhodan's place? She would have been glad to have escaped the light bodies at last and would have continued as quickly as possible on her way to her destination. The sooner it was reached the better for all those who shared in this undertaking.

And what did he do? He took time for a pause as if he were taking a walk or a hike and conducted for the amusement of an audience an experiment with the light bodies, the deadly danger of which had been demonstrated only too convincingly.

It was impossible to understand Rhodan – his restless energy, the austerity he displayed and expected from others, the lightning fast flexibility of his thoughts and his surprising gift to change the subject from a deadly serious topic to something almost foolish or even mischievous.

Thora shook her head and set the *Stardust* in motion.

Cautiously, as once before, the vessel descended into the swirling tempest of Gol's atmosphere and gradually lost altitude. Thora knew what to watch for. Below two hundred and fifty miles altitude they faced the danger that the light bodies would begin to gobble up the rich energy of the ship's protective screen. Evidently they had no difficulty rising two hundred and fifty miles high from the surface of the giant planet.

The modified structure sensor had been installed in the meantime. They could apply a value of two megawatts for the transmission; that was all the sensitive oscillation cycles could absorb.

Thora stared at the small box.

Rhodan! He had dismantled an Arkonide structure sensor and rebuilt it in such a fashion that he achieved something which was not even known to Arkonide physics.

'Altitude two hundred and fifty miles, ma'am!' announced the range finder officer.

Thora was startled.

The danger zone began – and her fears.

'The *Stardust*!' murmured Deringhouse.

A pale white image slid from above onto the observation screen. Rhodan had switched off the searchlight since it was useless anyway and watched the picture which became clearer as the *Stardust* sank lower.

Thora had encountered no difficulties. Unimpeded, the ship had descended above the valley and was now drifting down with minimum velocity.

Rhodan had instructed Thora to emit the infrared

light in diffuse rays to illuminate the scene and it soon proved to have been very good advice.

Diffuse light was only a very weak source of energy and was dispersed isotropically without preferring any one direction. The stimulation to ingest the diffuse radiation of the infrared lights was too slight for the light bodies to get moving.

The scene was as clear as Rhodan could have wished. For the first time he was in a position to overlook the entire round basin and to see its impressive size. The diameter appeared to be close to twenty miles and everywhere – east, west and north – were almost vertical walls, some with mountains towering above them and others ascending to a ridge and forming glistening mesas covered with methane ice.

The basin was inundated with the army of light bodies. Their light was intense enough so that they stood out in the shine of the searchlights. They remained motionless.

'That's enough, Thora!' said Rhodan when the *Stardust* had come down to about three miles. 'Turn on the set!'

'I'm pressing the switch!' responded Thora.

The success was instantaneous and complete as everyone had hoped but nobody had seriously dared to believe.

Momentarily the mass of lights started to move. In contrast to the protective screens and neutralizing fields of the ship and vehicles the oscillations of the transmitter were of a higher order which they sensed immediately and to which they promptly reacted.

For a few seconds the movement gave the appearance of being aimless. Then a big hole opened up in the middle of the field of light bodies and increased rapidly in all directions.

'They're fleeing!' shouted Deringhouse triumphantly. 'They really beat it!'

There was no longer any doubt about it. Thora was sweeping indiscriminately across the energy creatures and caused panics at numerous spots simultaneously.

The flanks of the army reached the walls of the valley basin – and vanished inside. Solid matter was no obstacle for the energy bodies. As they raced towards the mountain walls by the thousands with amazing speed and disappeared, the walls seemed to glow from the inside. The glow lasted a while after the last of the phantoms had fled, then gradually paled and was finally completely gone.

The valley basin was empty.

'It's all right, Thora!' said Rhodan quietly. 'You may land in the valley.'

They watched the landing of the *Stardust*. Then Rhodan urged everybody to depart again.

He was just about to give the order when Tanaka Seiko woke up. Rhodan heard him moan and turned around.

Tanaka held his head and looked questioningly at Rhodan.

'What's that?' Tanaka asked.

'What's what?'

'This humming and buzzing. Can't you hear it?'

Rhodan shook his head. 'What could it be?' he asked.

Tanaka listened closely and it was his turn to shake his head.

'It sounds like a swarm of excited hornets. I could swear there's one in the neighbourhood but that's nonsense, of course.'

Rhodan thought about it a moment.

Doubtlessly Tanaka 'heard' something thanks to his parapsychological capabilities. If that was the case there remained only two possible sources for the noise after Thora had switched off the transmitter: the unknown who concealed himself in the mountain or the escaped light bodies.

'Can you understand anything?' Rhodan inquired further.

'No, sir. It's just a noise.'

Rhodan thought it must be the light bodies. He considered them to be unintelligent and if they uttered any sounds which were commensurate with the energy structure of their bodies they were bound to be meaningless.

Like a swarm of excited hornets—

Rhodan kept mulling over the matter. He had to come to a decision and the sooner he did it the better it would be for him and his men.

He reached for the microphone.

'Khrest and Bell! I want you both to return to the *Stardust*. I'm not very sure that we've put the light bodies to flight indefinitely and I'd like you to help Thora if another attack comes.'

Bell protested.

'You're painting too black a picture,' he called back, quite upset. 'I think we've spoiled their appetite for good.'

'That's what you think!' answered Rhodan. 'No more

discussions. You'll drive back with Khrest. And now listen closely!'

'Yes?'

'You both will have to get busy and build as quickly as possible a second transmitter of the same type as the modified structure sensor. At this time you'll have an opportunity to disconnect the protective screens and to produce a sufficient amount of antiparticles for the second oscillation cycle. The second transmitter will follow behind me in one of your two vehicles: I'll give you guide signals. The vehicle will be driven by Major Nyssen and only one other man will accompany him. Have I made myself clear?'

'Yes.'

'Okay. Get going!'

Rhodan waited until the other two vehicles turned around and disappeared over the slightly rounded edge of the northern mountain slope. He called Thora and asked her to prepare all necessary materials for the construction of a second transmitter.

Then he looked at his crew.

'Tanaka, how's the humming now?'

'The same as before, sir.'

Rhodan nodded.

'Anne, how about a little friendlier face. We've won a battle and should be glad about it.'

'But ...'

'No buts. We're close to our goal and when we've reached it, all our troubles will be over.'

That's said so easily, he thought. But there was no point in describing the difficulties of their situation to people who were afraid already. A good commander's foremost task was to instill courage and confidence in his crew.

He saw that Deringhouse looked at him with anticipation.

Rhodan's face broke into a grin.

'We're shoving off!' he said sternly and made the engine whine at the same time.

The next hour passed uneventfully – on board the *Stardust* as well as in Rhodan's caterpillar.

Khrest and Bell had reached the vessel and gone to work right away. Since Thora had prepared everything that could be done ahead of time and Khrest had already once before performed the same work as Rhodan's assistant, they believed they could finish the job in two or three hours. The capacity of this transmitter would be somewhat less than the first one, since they did not dare draw on the energy of the protection and neutralization screens for more than forty seconds for the production of antiparticles. Even this time span almost drove Khrest into a panic.

In the meantime Rhodan's vehicle had advanced at a brisk pace across the plateau. At the end of an hour they reached an embankment of sorts which formed an incline of fifteen feet and ran straight along the east-west direction as far as the eye could see.

Rhodan wondered about it. There was nothing to indicate the origin of the precise shape set in the middle of the plateau or what natural event had created it.

He drove the vehicle down the embankment and noticed that the ground below was a shade smoother than the one they travelled on heretofore.

He revved up the engine with full power and let the vehicle thunder across the level plain.

One hour later Bell reported from the *Stardust* that the transmitter had been completed and that it soon would be under way with Major Nyssen.

Rhodan felt somewhat relieved, although he had not seen any more light bodies in the meantime.

The *Stardust*, too, had so far remained undisturbed.

Major Nyssen regarded his mission as a lark. He had selected Captain Klein as companion, for which Klein was very grateful.

It took only a few minutes to traverse the basin where the phantoms had roamed a few hours ago, and they were pushing the vehicle up the mountain slops as fast as it would go.

Rhodan was the first to run out of luck. It was a rather ridiculous mishap but dangerous nevertheless.

Almost three hours had pased since he had sent Bell and Khrest back to the *Stardust*. The ground was still smooth and permitted Rhodan to proceed at top speed.

However, he had now to slow down rather abruptly as he suddenly had the feeling that the vehicle no longer responded properly to his steering.

He looked at the observation screen and watched the ground on which they travelled. He did not notice anything in particular. He reduced his speed even more – and then he saw it all of a sudden.

The ground underneath the vehicle was sinking!

It looked as if he drove on a tautly stretched cloth.

Rhodan stopped and racked his brains to figure out the

phenomenon. Deringhouse sidled up to him and also stared at the screen. The effect was now clearly discernible. The weight of the car caused the ground to form some kind of a dish which tapered out, as far as Deringhouse could see, about one hundred and fifty feet away.

Rhodan acted immediately. He gunned the engine and pulled the vehicle forward with a rough jolt.

'We're damn fools!' growled Rhodan. 'It's ice! We've been driving for an hour and a half on a frozen lake and nobody's noticed it.'

That explained the incline about which he had wondered. It was the shore of the lake.

Rhodan started to breathe easier when he saw that he approached a similar embankment to the south. It could be no more than eight hundred yards away, and if they were lucky—

No such luck!

The body of the vehicle reverberated with the acoustic waves and with surprising clarity transmitted the loud detonation with which the ice broke. The observation screen showed that the ice had developed cracks which became wider with alarming speed.

Then the picture slanted down. The vehicle started to capsize.

'Anne!' shouted Rhodan. 'Full power for the generators!'

The howling of the freewheeling engines was mixed with the roaring hum of the generators running at full power to reinforce the neutralizing field of the vehicle to keep it from sinking.

Rhodan knew that there was little hope. The vehicle was filled with air at normal pressure. But far more important than the volume was the weight of the vehicle's body, the generator and engine. Even if one considered that the density of the lake's methane was far greater than that of Terrestrial water and produced more buoyancy, there was no doubt that they would sink in a few minutes.

Had Rhodan known that the lake was less than fifty feet deep at this spot, he would have made no efforts to prevent the vehicle from sinking, since the vehicle's body was still able to withstand the pressure of compressed liquid methane at a depth of fifty feet.

The treads churned up the sluggish liquid and set it in motion. Rhodan kept the engine spinning at maximum speed in order to propel as much methane as possible from the front end of the car to the rear. Every little bit helped to push the car forward. Under the circumstances, every yard closer to the shore was worth a fortune.

Tanaka got set to operate the far ranging telecom transmitter for an emergency call to the *Stardust* in case Rhodan's radio was unable to span the distance. A few feet of liquid methane ruined the best radio communication if there was not sufficient energy available.

Rhodan watched the screen which was half covered with sluggishly moving methane. The other half showed the shore and safety. It had not come appreciably closer.

The neutralizing generators delayed the sinking but did not stop it altogether. The crazily swirling tracks imparted no measurable velocity against the viscous mass in which they threatened to drown.

Rhodan used his own set to call the *Stardust*. As yet it functioned faultlessly. The antenna still extended above the surface of the methane.

'We'll take off right away and fish you out!' Bell assured Rhodan.

'You'll have to hover closely above our vehicle and reinforce the neutralizing field of the ship till you can lift it out,' explained Rhodan quickly. 'It's the only way.'

'All right!' answered Bell. 'Have the stronger transmitter send us guide signals!'

Rhodan turned to Tanaka.

'Get the transmitter ...'

At this instant they felt a jolt. The vehicle groaned a little, rocked slightly and came to rest.

The observation screen showed only muddy methane except for an inch wide stripe at the upper edge.

'What was that?' asked Deringhouse breathlessly.

Rhodan started to laugh.

'We've touched ground!'

It took a while until they all realized it.

They were saved. The lake was only ten feet deep at this point. Four-fifths of the vehicle was in methane. But the treads grabbed the ground of the lake and pushed the vehicle forward.

Rhodan called the alarm off. Bell was relieved.

The vehicle proceeded like an icebreaker. Rhodan steered prudently and went ahead by taking advantage mainly of those places where the methane ice had already split.

In this manner it took him half an hour to surmount the last eight hundred yards to the shore. The vehicle emerged dripping from the lake and clambered up the embankment.

Rhodan wanted to say a few encouraging words to

his crew. However, the picture he saw on the visiscreen fascinated him.

Five hundred yards ahead a needle-like rock soared up high. That it was a needle, Rhodan only recognized after sweeping the searchlight a few times up and down the sides of the rock. The diameter was quite impressive and it evidently reached up way beyond the range of the searchlight. Rhodan remembered that the range finder on board the *Stardust* had made out the peak of a mountain only from a relatively low altitude. This indicated that the actual peak of the mountain was not a wide object – as, for instance, this needle.

Could it be *the mountain?*

Suddenly Tanaka Seiko began to scream. Rhodan whirled around. The face of the Japanese was distorted in pain and he pressed his hands against his temples.

Then the Japanese abruptly stopped his screaming, his hands dropped and he stared with a look of alleviated feelings.

'What's going on?' asked Rhodan.

'A message, sir.'

'What did it say?'

'It said: "You are on the right way. Keep going! Are you endowed with the higher knowledge?"'

In answer Rhodan merely growled. He had not expected to hear from the unknown again at this time. Nevertheless it was comforting. The cluster of mountains was of huge dimensions and he had to be thankful to be told that he was on the right path.

The carrier rolled leisurely towards the needle rock.

Rhodan gave the information to the *Stardust* and to Major Nyssen in his vehicle.

'The humming's getting stronger, sir,' said Tanaka suddenly.

At the same time Rhodan recognized a peculiar pattern on the north side of the tremendous needle which was now a mere six hundred feet away.

The needle was, as all rock formations in this world, covered with methane and ammonia ice. Because of the steep slope, however, it was only a thin layer which did not entirely hide the more distinct features of the rock's surface.

One could easily perceive a groove in the shape of a horseshoe, the two ends of which started at the foot of the rock and converged at a height of sixty feet. The ice was also lodged in the groove but it reflected the light of the infrared searchlight at a different angle, which made it stand out clearly against the environment.

Rhodan believed that he was able to explain the groove.

'There's the gate!' he said earnestly. 'Anne, I assume that it takes telekinetic knack to open it. Please apply your higher knowledge!'

He turned around and smiled at Anne.

Deringhouse added: 'And give it a good try, Anne! Because here come our friends from the other dimension!'

Rhodan spun around again.

A whole company of dancing, scintillating energy bodies approached from the right. They seemed to know their goal. They were marching straight towards the horseshoe-shaped gate in the side of the mountain. They would reach it not later than the caterpillar.

'The heck with this weather!' Nyssen growled, annoyed.

The past few minutes the storm had become more violent. The vehicle which was provided only with a neutralizing field for gravity was fairly helpless against the elements. Only its extraordinary weight and the fact that it was rather low to the ground and did not offer much of an area of resistance to the storm prevented it from flying away.

Nyssen apprised the *Stardust* of the storm. The *Stardust* had not even noticed it.

Nyssen would have had to be more familiar with the high pressure dynamics of this world to realize that, due to the enormous pressure and extreme gravity on Gol, there was no such thing as great meteorological areas. The storm was continuous but the variations of its intensity were restricted to a few square miles of its surface. Beyond these limits no change in the weather could be noted. It was the same with temperature fluctuations.

'It's getting colder,' complained Klein, who was monitoring the measuring dials.

'I can tell,' answered Nyssen, avoiding an icicle which had just begun to grow up in front of the vehicle.

Suddenly the terrain became uneven. Mounds, boulders and veritable hills sprang up from the ground and blocked Nyssen's view. He increased his speed to escape the maze of new formations as quickly as possible but was forced to slow down again after a few moments. The danger of a collision was too great.

As the vehicle was evading a man-size piece of ice, another mountain of frozen methane formed incredibly fast in front of them. Klein noted the outside temperature of minus 330 °F. No wonder the methane was condensed by the ton from the atmosphere, but it was astonishing to see the mountains grow before one's eyes.

Nyssen cursed and stopped the car. He backtracked a little in order to make a left turn. He moved a few feet and got stuck in the back. The rear screen sector showed a second mountain growing up behind him. In addition to the obstacle at his right, which he was trying to circumvent, another one was shooting up from the ground on his left with terrifying rapidity.

'Damn it!' Nyssen swore, utterly disgusted. 'We're stuck!'

He called the *Stardust* and described his situation.

'We'll get you out!' promised Bell. 'Rhodan appears to have reached his destination, judging from the latest conversations we've overheard. It won't do any harm to leave here and come up to you.'

'All right, sir,' replied Nyssen, a little more at ease. 'We'll wait."

The storm had ceased since the four walls of ice held it back.

Nyssen kept watching the observation screen till his eyes hurt. Finally he leaned back and relaxed.

Klein was busy with his instruments. He seemed to be profoundly interested in what was happening outside. Nobody had yet observed such low temperatures on Gol.

Neither of them watched the generator box in the rear of the car which was separated only by a plastic panel from the main compartment.

The interior was illuminated by a single small light –

weak so it would not interefre with the observation of the screen.

All of a sudden Nyssen had the impression that the light turned brighter. Wondering about it he turned around and it was at the same moment that Klein shouted:

'There . . . !'

Nyssen saw it at once. A small glowing cloud extruded from the centre of the panel which closed off the generator compartment. It was wavering back and forth and its light increased from second to second.

Nyssen and Klein sat, scared stiff, without stirring in their seats.

The cloud did not seem to know what it wanted. It moved here and there without leaving the panel. But its luminosity gained continually.

Nyssen felt that an invisible force pressed him down on his seat. It took a little while till he realized what was going on.

'It's drawing the power from the generators!' he yelled.

Klein jumped up.

He looked as if he felt threatened by the cloud of light. It began to shrink again and vanished in a short time. Klein dropped back into his seat and groaned as he became aware that his weight had doubled.

'Remove the panel!' ordered Nyssen.

The cover was held by four screws which were easily unfastened. Klein was able to unscrew them without leaving his seat. The plate toppled forward.

Nyssen stared into the generator compartment.

The generator for the engine and all auxiliary motors

was a shapeless lump of metal.

The protective screen generator was damaged but apparently still partly functioned.

'Check it!' he snapped at Klein. 'We've got to know whether it'll hold up.'

Klein crawled back, moaning, and examined the generator. It took some time. Then he awkwardly turned his head and said over his shoulder:

'It's in pretty bad shape, sir. It can conk out any time.'

Nyssen gulped.

'Well now ...'

The carrier was immobilized. The hyper-transmitter, because of which they had undertaken this trip, was useless as it was connected to the drive generator. The light was burned out and the illumination in the interior was furnished solely by the observation screen which was connected to the protective screen generator.

Nyssen turned it off.

He knew the telecom received its power from the protective screen, and therefore he was able to contact the *Stardust*.

He was reaching clumsily for the microphone when another jolt hit the vehicle. Klein and Nyssen grunted simultaneously. Nyssen's outstretched hand dropped and smacked against the steering wheel.

The gravity had grown even more severe; the generator was losing energy. Nyssen estimated the gravity inside the carrier to three G's.

Then he stretched his hand farther out and grabbed the microphone. It had become very heavy but it was still working.

He called the *Stardust.*

But the *Stardust* gave no answer.

'We'll take off!' Reginald Bell had just announced.

Then he issued the routine commands from his console to initiate the starting procedure.

But the *Stardust* did not move.

Bell was sure that he had not made any mistakes. Anyone authorized to command this vessel could not make mistakes.

Besides him there was Thora in the Control Centre and a few other men who could possibly be useful under the circumstances.

Bell quickly countermanded his orders and stopped everything.

Without showing the alarm he felt, he called the engineer.

The engineer answered immediately and by now Thora had also noticed that something had gone awry.

'Anything wrong?'

Bell shook his head.

'I'm going down to the Technical Guidance Section,' he said. 'Wait a few minutes, I'll be back right away.'

Then he was gone.

He covered the considerable distance from the Control Centre to the Technical Guidance Section in record time. He stormed along the moving belts in the hallways and struggled with the reduced drag of the antigrav elevators.

The Guidance Section was located about six hundred feet below the Control Centre. Bell squeezed through the door which opened reluctantly and surveyed the room full of switch consoles.

Nobody was there.

The Guidance Section was closed off at one side with a transparent wall behind which the room containing the generators was located. Bell looked through the wall and behind the shining, colossal atomic HHe-piles, the protective screen generators and the array of auxiliary installations.

The protective screen generators were working and produced a slight hum which affected the separating wall and was audible in the Technical Guidance Section. Nobody was to be seen in the generator room. It was empty and – except for the slight hum – quiet.

With resounding steps Bell stomped to the other end of the Guidance Section and released a door behind which a small moving belt led down to the level of the generator room. He stepped on the belt and moved down.

A nauseating sense of danger threatened to overwhelm him as the belt carried him down to the huge room. He pulled his weapon and released the safety catch. So far there was nothing in sight at which to shoot.

The atomic piles and generators were arranged in long rows. The walkways between them were a few yards wide. However, since the installations were sixty feet and higher, the view of the room was quite obstructed.

The feeling of impending danger grew as Bell left the moving belt which stopped running behind him. He entered the first walkway. Left and right stood the atomic piles for sector A drive. Behind them were the two protective screen generators for sector A and then a long row of auxiliary equipment. This row was two hundred and fifty feet long.

The protective screen generators were functioning. Bell examined the dials and found everything in order.

What annoyed him was the fact that he could not see anyone in the entire room. The Technical Section had instructions to keep a guard of at least ten men to watch the generators at all times. In spite of the obstructed view he should have seen at least one of the guards.

Bell marched on. His steps sounded hollow and muffled. He walked firmer than usual and did not realize that he did it only to hear another noise above the haunting hum.

He was standing in front of the two protective screen generators when he heard an odd noise. He did not know where it came from but it sounded like a series of clanging bells.

Then, before he could counteract, a jolt ripped through the ship and made him lose his balance so that he was hurled violently to the floor. When he tried to get up again he saw that the floor slanted down.

He quickly got up on his feet. He bent over to pick up his weapon, which had fallen from his hand, and as he raised his head again, he saw it clearly.

His thinking had become slow and cumbersome as in a dream.

It's only one, he thought. *At least so far—*

It peeped out from behind the far corner of the walkway, flowed like a cloud of heavy fumes and then moved slowly around the corner.

They've discovered a new trick, reflected Bell bitterly, Why satisfy their hunger out in the field of the protective screen when it was just as easy for them to penetrate the walls and to gorge themselves at the source.

He had already before witnessed with his own eyes that solid walls were no hindrance for them.

Instinctively he raised his hand with the weapon.

The glowing cloud came closer.

It had tapped the atomic piles, Bell thought, which was the reason he could not start. Moreover, they had drained one of the generators, causing the vessel to tip over.

If I don't finish it off, it'll cost us our necks.

Something made him turn around and look back down the gangway.

It was a second light body. It also proceeded around the corner onto the walk and came towards him.

He lost his nerve and began to shoot. He struck the phantom which he had spied first. That seemed to make the thing very happy. It brightened up at the spot where he hit. It also approached him with increased speed.

Screaming wildly in fear and anger, Bell whirled around and shot at the other intruder. It had the same effect and then the glowing clouds engulfed him.

With amazement he noticed a prickly feeling which ran through his body as though he had come into contact with a low voltage source. The sensation was titillating – at least for a while. But then it became stronger. He opened his eyes wide and saw that the light bodies blocked his sight completely. He saw nothing but a glowing, swaying amorphous mass.

The pain became worse. It grew and grew; Bell's head began to drone until the pain was finally alleviated by the bliss of unconsciousness.

Thora was unable to cope with the events she failed to understand.

She tried to advise Rhodan of the situation but he did not respond. Neither did Nyssen, who was waiting somewhere out there for the help of the *Stardust*.

The observation screens had turned black after the ship was suddenly jolted and the floors were inclined.

We're besieged, speculated Thora. *They're absorbing all energy produced by the vessel.*

She did not suspect that the foreign bodies had already invaded the ship.

She wanted to call Khrest and wondered why he had not come to her aid before when a second blow shook the ship.

Concurrently Thora felt the same leaden heaviness she had first experienced when the light bodies had attacked the first time.

The generators were no longer working with full efficiency.

She heard the people around her yell and curse. The light began to flicker and died out after hesitating shortly.

Thora sank to the floor under the terrific weight induced by the extreme gravity and moved no more. She was not yet unconscious but it seemed best, under the circumstances, to lose herself in her own helplessness.

'Have you got it?' asked Rhodan.

'In a minute,' panted Anne Sloane. 'There's a duct in the rock and . . . oh, nothing!'

According to what Anne had found so far by applying her telekinetic senses, there were at least a few hundred ducts the size of an arm running through the rock in any and all directions, ending nowhere.

Anne had to search through all of them to locate the mechanism which opened the gate.

But until then . . .

Deringhouse made impatient noises. He had taken over Tanaka's job since the Japanese suffered again with intolerable head pains from the time the light bodies had appeared once more. Rhodan had been unable to contact the *Stardust* or Nyssen with his low-powered telecom. For ten minutes Deringhouse attempted it with the considerably stronger transmitter – with just as little success.

The army of light bodies was posted in front of the horseshoe gate and seemed to wait for something.

Rhodan was afraid that Anne might lose her strength before she could find the mechanism. He also feared that the *Stardust* had been attacked for the second time and that Nyssen had run into trouble.

Anne's head jerked forward. She looked unreal.

'I've got it!' she said with a low moan.

Rhodan swivelled around in his seat.

'Don't open it yet,' he told her. 'Wait a minute!'

The vehicle rumbled on. It had stopped three hundred feet away from the gate; now it was two hundred and fifty, only two hundred . . .

The light bodies did not move. They blocked the gate and Rhodan worried about the question of how many of them would enter the mountain when Anne opened the gate.

. . . One hundred feet, fifty feet . . .

'Open!' bellowed Rhodan.

Anne gnashed her teeth.

Nothing happened for half a second. Then a small crack formed at the bottom where the horseshoe met the ground. Rhodan watched and saw that the gate was pulled up like a stage curtain.

He estimated the speed of the car and the height of the opening at the time the car reached the entrance. For a second he was tempted to brake because the gate was moving too slowly; but then he gave up the idea.

He did not have time to watch the light bodies. There was a sharp knock as the roof of the vehicle rammed under the edge of the door and a loud and terrifying bang.

They were through!

'Shut the gate!' hollered Rhodan.

He drove around in a wide circle without watching where he was going and turned the carrier at 90°. He felt reassured, looking at the observation screen and noting that the door had closed again and that, evidently, it all happened too fast for the light bodies. Due to their slow reaction time, they had not realized quickly enough what was taking place.

There was a slight rustle at his side and then a plop.

Anne had fainted after the exertions of the last fifteen minutes.

Rhodan wanted to say something, but at this moment the observation screen flashed so brightly that they all were blinded and had to close their eyes.

Rhodan blinked. Cautiously, between half-closed eyelids, he studied the picture on the screen.

He found himself in a hall. It was circular with a diameter of about a hundred feet and fairly high.

The light source which illuminated the scene was

meant for eyes that were used to the blue-white splendour of Vega, not for human eyes.

What surprised Rhodan was that the hall was completely empty except for one not especially large object.

Rhodan recognized it. It was an impulsator such as they had already seen once before in another factory-like hall when they first attempted to track down the unknown stranger. At that time Bell had ventured too close and was carried off in an iridescent energy spiral.

This device called an impulsator effected transitions through hyperspace. The person to be transmitted did not have to sit or stand at a particular place nor was it necessary to be connected to it. The transmitter functioned with a directed transport-impulse and was a refinement of the set which the Ferrons used.

This one here was larger than the one they had seen in the factory hall. At least five times as big. Nevertheless, it looked lost in the vast hall.

Rhodan pulled up. The same gravity prevailed in the hall as on the surface of Gol.

The vehicle suddenly began to vibrate. Rhodan had noticed that the steering wheel had started to move and looked for the cause. He glanced at the observation screen and saw that the impulsator had wandered off downward.

The transmitter? Going down?

It was the carrier which had moved. It hovered a couple of feet above the ground and appeared to be rising steadily.

'Do you see that, Deringhouse?'

'Yes, sir.'

'Regulate the neutralizing generator. Somebody's

turning off the gravity. Adjust the generator accordingly so that we won't fly away.'

Deringhouse attended skilfully to his task. A few anxious minutes passed during which the car either just touched the ground or floated a mite above it.

'That's it, sir,' reported Deringhouse finally. 'It's stopped.'

The vehicle had its own gravity indicator. The gravity outside amounted to one point two G.

Rhodan closed his helmet. Deringhouse did the same as well as Tanaka Seiko, who had regained full control of himself after they had left the light bodies behind. Anne was still unconscious. They closed her helmet without her noticing it.

They had to get out. The vehicle had an exit but no airlock since nobody had expected that they would have to leave the carrier outside the *Stardust*.

What was awaiting them outside, they did not know. Perhaps an atmosphere they could breathe, perhaps another unfit to breathe or maybe none at all.

'Let's go!' ordered Rhodan.

He opened the hatch. It was not difficult at all, just a barely noticeable little push.

The hall had an atmosphere and the pressure differential between the atmosphere in the hall and the vehicle was not particularly great. Of what did the atmosphere consist?

Rhodan did not take any chances. The helmets and the spacesuits remained closed.

He turned his attention to the impulsator. Apparently it functioned on the same principle as the one they had encountered earlier at the other place. It had a row of coloured buttons, a regulator for destination, a space-angle system and a target screen.

All this Rhodan knew how to operate himself. He had learned it. He was able to select the destination and to review it.

But the one thing he could not do was to activate the transmitter.

He had learned at the prior occasion that it required the telekinetic capability of a mutant. There was no other way to close the contact.

Rhodan pushed the buttons with the hard gloves of his protective suit. The screen lit up brightly. The picture was sharp and clear whichever range he chose, much brighter, as if shown in infrared light.

He scouted unknown areas on Gol's surface. Level plains of methane ice crystals and wild, craggy mountains reaching up to endless heights. He turned the target knob in a direction he guessed to be north. Evidently, it was not quite correct, but it took only a slight rotation and the push of a button which adjusted the range to bring the *Stardust* into view.

Deringhouse loudly expressed his surprise.

'Sir, the vessel is leaning!'

Rhodan nodded. He had expected it after the communication with the ship was broken.

The inclined position of the ship was not significant. If that was all that had happened, the *Stardust* was built to take it.

Something else attracted Rhodan's attention.

The visual target system was evidently equipped with a wide-angle lens. The observation screen not only showed the *Stardust* but also the lake in which Rhodan's vehicle had almost sunk, the entire route they had travelled from the valley basin and rows of ice formations which had sprung up north of the lake shore as a result of a weather change.

'Miss Sloane is coming to,' said the Japanese softly.

Rhodan glanced at her. Anne stirred.

She alone was capable of activating the impulsator.

Is that what we're searching for? Rhodan asked himself. *A transmitter?*

He never had had a clear idea of what was waiting for them on Gol. Another clue, he believed. A sign for the next stretch of the path they had undertaken to explore.

Was it the transmitter? Did they receive the tips through it?

It looked like it. The hall contained nothing except the transmitter. Rhodan did not know what would happen if Anne operated it.

But he trusted the unknown who knew the situation to which those who were following his trail were exposed and the transmitter was bound to be a safeguard against the perils which lurked in this world.

Anne rose to her knees. Rhodan helped her to get up.

'Have you recovered?' asked Rhodan solicitously.

Anne nodded.

'It'll have to be all right.'

She smiled through her helmet's faceplate, which was clear as glass.

'Okay. You know the mechanism. The target's set. Start it up.'

Anne closed her eyes. Rhodan tensed his muscles, anticipating the acute pain which had to come.

And it came, indeed.

In a tenth of a second the painful brightness faded. Rhodan was gripped by intense pains and he would have screamed if it had been possible during the transition.

For how long—

CHAPTER SEVEN

BEYOND THE GALAXY

– An endless time.

Nobody could judge the human sense of time during a transition. But it seemed to Rhodan that no prior transition had taken as long as this one.

Hours seemed to pass till the spasmodic pain – indicative of the end of the transition – began again and light appeared once more before the faceplate of his helmet.

If that wasn't—!

There was a jolt as if he had been pushed down but he stood firmly on his legs.

Deringhouse arrived beside him, lost his balance and brushed against him. Behind Deringhouse appeared Tanaka Seiko and Anne Sloane.

And the place in which they had landed was the Command Centre of the *Stardust*.

Or was it?

Thora was lying on the floor. She raised herself up on her arms, lifted her head and looked around in a daze. Her eyes caught Rhodan's legs, followed them up and she recognized his face.

'You . . . ?'

At this moment of utter surprise Rhodan again displayed his capabilities which had nearly earned him the reputation of a monster among the psychologists of the scientific staff at the Nevada proving grounds during the last phase of his test pilot training, years ago.

They had arrived in a completely inexplicable manner from the hall in the mountain on board the *Stardust*. Good and fine! It was a mystery about which they could rack their brains later. More important was—

'Everything in order on board?' he asked gruffly.

Thora stood up.

'How ... how did you ... ?'

'Is everything in order?' repeated Rhodan with increased emphasis.

Thora stared at him with open mouth.

'No ...' she stammered after a while. '... Bell ... the light bodies ...'

'Where's Bell?'

Thora had to think hard.

'In the Technical Guidance Section!'

Rhodan turned to Deringhouse.

'Take care of the Command Centre. Find out what happened. I'll be back right away.'

Bell was found. He was lying in the generator room – unconscious and in electrical shock. He received treatment and was up and around again half an hour later.

He recounted what he had been up against, whereupon a search was made for the light bodies, but there were none to be found anywhere in the vessel.

A few minutes after Bell had rendered his account, Major Nyssen and Captain Klein showed up at the Command Centre. They were both rather excited. They reported that their damaged vehicle was locked in by mountains of ice. A light body had raided the carrier and had completely destroyed the drive generator as well as part of the protective screen generator. The latest impression they had gleaned from Gol was that the gravity had mounted to approximately ten G's. They had already made their peace with the world in their minds since the *Stardust* gave no answer and then—

The tale was incoherent. They had the impression that their vehicle had gone into a transition. When they had regained consciousness after some time, they had found themselves and the carrier in one of the *Stardust's* airlocks. They had climbed out with shaking knees, ridden up to the Command Centre and here they were!

The *Stardust's* machinery was again performing faultlessly. The intrusion of the light bodies had left no permanent damage.

Where had the ghosts gone?

That's the wrong question, thought Rhodan

Where are we?

The wide observation screens of the *Stardust* depicted a space never before seen by Rhodan nor Khrest and Thora.

The points of lights the stars were shining onto the observation screen could be counted. There were maybe fifty or sixty of them in the space sector.

Anyone who had ever looked up to the sky with the shimmering galaxy of myriads of lights knew what the picture portended.

When they had finished the transition which the impulsator in the mountain hall on Gol had triggered, the *Stardust* had landed in a sector of space which was beyond the galaxy they knew as home.

A sky with sixty forlorn stars did not exist in the Milky Way.

Rhodan had deduced it at once and harboured – for a few minutes – the foolish hope that Khrest might know where they had been thrust. But Khrest's Arkonide knowledge was no greater than Rhodan's. He was not familiar with this region of space but he patiently tackled the task of detecting, with the aid of maps, a known sign for the orientation of the *Stardust.*

In the midst of this distressing uncertainty Tanaka received a message from the unknown mentor. The Japanese saw a glowing ball suspended in the middle of the Command Centre and became terribly frightened, believing at first that it was a light body.

Nobody except him, however, saw the ball nor did anyone else understand the message it conveyed:

'*You have been warned! Now find the world where the co-ordinates are secured. Remember that you cannot return home if you do not know the right way. Your goal is far!*'

He translated it and Rhodan nodded in assent.

Khrest endeavoured to identify a sign of recognition.

After calm had returned and nothing else could be done while they waited for Khrest's results, Rhodan recapped the events which had occurred on Gol.

He had some very attentive listeners, consisting of all those who had actively taken part in the events he described. There was, for instance, the engineer who, together with his twelve men guarding the generators, had been rendered unconscious by the light bodies and shoved into a corner of the generator room.

'Gol is a world,' Rhodan began, 'which differs somewhat from normal conditions. It has an average density of one hundred and fifty grams per cubic centimetre. This is more than the density of osmium, the heaviest metal we know.

'Therefore, Gol must be something like a cold sun – even though it circles Vega like a planet. In its interior must be gravity fields which do not conform to Newtonian principles but must have other causes.

'The light bodies appear to be a result of the special nature of this planet. They probably originate at the core of Gol which is in a non-Newtonian sphere of gravity.

'They're not very intelligent, meaning no more intelligent than, for example, a dog or a cat. They are, shall I say, individual energy or energized individuals.

'You know what I mean. Our language doesn't have words to describe such a thing as energy bodies.

'When we dislodged them from the valley basin – with the aid of the revamped transmitter whose oscillation proved to be very detrimental to them – they behaved just like a swarm of disturbed wasps. They regrouped and returned for a renewed attack. In doing so, they took a different tack than we expected and we were tricked by them.

'They penetrated the *Stardust* before anybody noticed it. They encroached, or rather one of them did, on Nyssen's vehicle and ruined the drive generator and therewith the source of current for the second hyper-transmitter which Nyssen carried. They also blocked our way but didn't get anywhere with that.'

He paused a moment.

'That,' he concluded, 'is about all we know about the light bodies, and part of it is strictly conjecture. It would be very interesting to learn more about them but we now have to follow another way.'

His listeners had lowered their heads and were collecting their thoughts.

They had entered a world which surpassed the imagination of humans and Arkonides as well. They had been rescued in a manner which was so peculiar as to be almost laughable.

Most of them considered the journey to Gol rather unenlightening. Those who had a better grasp of the events realized they had learned at least two things from this undertaking:

There were more beings in the universe than the mind could picture. The imagination of Mother Nature had not run dry when she made humans, Arkonides, Fantan people, Ferrons, Topides and others as yet unimagined by man, and unmet. Nature had created beings not of flesh and blood and assigned them to an abode in space of a higher order. The universe held an endless variety of sentient forms and anyone who thought that after a sojourn in space he could no longer encounter anything new was badly mistaken.

Secondly:

They were on the track of an unknown being who possessed technical powers beyond comprehension. By means of a comparatively tiny apparatus he had teleported a spaceship – the crowning scientific achievement of their technology to date – together with a group of four people and a heavy transportation vehicle, all into one place.

Perhaps the unknown one would one day offer the

solution when they reached him. *If* they reached him. Perhaps he would disclose the meaning of the game of wits in which he made Rhodan and his men trace his track through space and time.

Perhaps—

The hatch opened and Khrest entered.

Rhodan regarded the ancient Arkonide.

Khrest began uncertainly: 'I believe I've found something. But, please – don't rejoice too soon. I can't say for sure.'

Rhodan rose, walked over to the alien scientist with a smile on his face.

'Cheer up!' he said in a tone inspiring optimism. 'We've tackled tough challenges together before. Let's welcome one more!'